THE ALLURE

THE ALLURE

JACKIE KING-SCOTT

© 2003 by
JACKIE KING-SCOTT

Library of Congress Cataloging-in-Publication Data

King-Scott, Jackie, 1950-
 The allure / by Jackie King-Scott
   p. cm.
 ISBN 0-8024-1562-8
1. Separated people—Fiction. I. Title

PS3611.I59A78 2003
813'.54—dc21

2003013891

1 3 5 7 9 10 8 6 4 2

Printed in the United States of America

I dedicate this book to a man who without complaint has taken a backseat to the time it took to write it and his active role in helping me meet deadlines.

I dedicate this book to a man who has displayed a servant's heart as he waited on me while I sat for months with a broken leg, unable to do anything except write.

I dedicate this book to a quiet, yet passionate man who loves the Lord and his wife, and is commited to the call God has placed on her life through her writing.

I dedicate this book, to my husband, sent by God, Louis Scott.

Acknowledgements

A special thank you to Kathy Blonk (my sister) and her husband Bob Blonk for the multitude of information you provided about the cruise. You not only furnished itinerary information, your fabulous pictures and detailed descriptions lent a human element to that chapter, giving a sense of feeling and purpose to the entire cruise.

Thank you, Annette Cullors for your help and encouragement in the critical Fruit segments. Thanks to your enthusiasm, Dr. Matthews took on exuberance and life, thereby getting across the message of how critical the Fruit of the Spirit is to the success of marriages.

Menaja Obinali, your literary and editing skills are unsurpassed. You listen for the slightest nuance or misplaced comma, something I am very adept at doing. I thank you for your instant help whenever I call, and I thank you for the immense contribution you have given to the maturation of this fictional yet true account of a couple whose marriage is on the brink of failure.

I thank you all for your unswerving belief in the grace of God, and for your conviction that God can speak through fiction.

CONTENTS

One

THE ENCOUNTER

The ball hurtled through the warm spring air like a guided missile, heading straight for Valerie Townsend's face. She threw up her hands to protect herself, dropping the pile of magazines she'd been carrying.

"I'm sorry, ma'am!" a little boy yelled breathlessly, running hard toward her. "I didn't mean for it to go toward you! I'm sorry!"

"That's OK," she assured the boy, bending to retrieve the fallen magazines.

"Here, let me get those for you," said a voice that was definitely not that of a boy. Valerie straightened in the direction of the voice and was surprised to look into one of the warmest pairs of eyes she'd ever seen. The gorgeous, gray-green eyes belonged to a tall, athletically built man who offered her a wide smile. She admired the way his thick wavy hair shone in the sun.

The man scooped up the magazines and handed them to her. "Are you all right?" he asked, a note of concern in his voice.

Valerie smiled in return. "Thanks, I'm fine. My arm took the blow, so there's no harm done."

He extended his hand in one smooth motion. "Curtis Chambers," he offered. She gave his hand a quick squeeze. "Hi, I'm Valerie Townsend."

Valerie tucked her magazines under her arm and turned to continue her search for a shady park bench, but Curtis wanted to continue the conversation.

"Do you come here often?" he asked. "I haven't seen you in this part of the park before."

"Actually, I just started," Valerie said. "I've been looking for a place to think and read."

That was an understatement, and she knew it. She was looking for a place to escape the stifling animosity that hung in the air between her and her husband, John. Even though they shared a spacious home, it sometimes felt like the world wasn't large enough for the two of them to get along. It was easy enough to ignore each other during the week when they both worked, but lately weekends had become tense and unpleasant. Just a few minutes ago, she'd yelled at him about just how sick he made her sometimes. Then she'd grabbed an armful of magazines and left to find some peace and quiet.

It wasn't that she and John had had some disruptive ugliness between them, really. But after seven years, their marriage had lost some of its glow. A lot of its glow. Things had been just fine during the first five. In fact, there'd been times when she'd never expected their honeymoon stage to end. But it had come to an abrupt end after they'd been unable to start a family. And after her miscarriage a year ago and the depression that followed, her marriage had begun to unravel like a poorly crafted pair of baby booties. And, when Valerie was honest with herself, she wasn't sure she cared much about knitting it back together.

"Well, I'm glad I came this way today," Curtis said. His voice jolted Valerie from her thoughts.

"I'm sorry?" she said, asking him to repeat himself.

He eyed her appreciatively. "I said, I'm glad I came this

way today. I was on my way to a rehearsal with my band and decided to take a shortcut through the park."

Valerie noticed the guitar case at his feet. "You play guitar?" she asked.

"Bass," he said, smiling again. "But only for the Lord."

She felt a little embarrassed at the way her heart skipped at his words: "Only for the Lord." It was nice enough that he was a Christian, but she wondered whether she was happy for him or for herself. Why was she suddenly so intrigued by this stranger?

"Well, thanks again for saving my face," she said, turning again to leave.

Curtis picked up his guitar case.

"Maybe I'll see you again," Curtis said. "I come through here every week when I go to band rehearsal, and sometimes I jog here." He paused, and held her eyes with his. "I'll be looking for you," he said. "See you next time."

"Nice to meet you," she said, hoping he couldn't tell how flustered she was by the way he focused so intently on her. "Bye."

He strode off, rounded a curve and was out of her sight. Was he flirting with her, flashing her that stunning smile?

Valerie sat down on the park bench and wondered if there were some reason she'd run into Curtis at that particular time. He certainly was intriguing.

❋ ❋ ❋

Valerie sat in her bedroom three Saturdays later, watching the pouring rain. She was thoroughly disappointed that she could not go to the park that day. All week she'd thought about the last two encounters with Curtis. Now it would be another week before she could possibly see him again. Their meetings had been harmless, Valerie told herself. They just met at her park bench and chatted. Curtis talked to her about his hopes for the band, and she told him about her work as an administrative assistant to the director of the local museum of African-American art and culture. Valerie was flattered by the interest he took in her work, and she enjoyed listening to his stories.

Several times over the last few weeks, she'd found herself wondering why God would allow this handsome, friendly man to come into her life. She'd been unhappy in her marriage for some time; was Curtis God's answer to her prayer to be free of it? After all, God wouldn't want her to be so unhappy for so long, would He?

Valerie laughed at herself, feeling foolish. In her mind's eye, the two of them had dated, she had divorced John, and they were headed for the altar. *It's only been three weeks,* she reasoned, *and besides, he's not interested in me that way. We're just two people who really hit it off.*

She decided to do her weekend chores, just in case the sun came out that afternoon. She washed clothes, did some grocery shopping and ran a load of dishes. When the sun did emerge from the clouds, Valerie was ready to go. She chose a casual pantsuit and a chic pair of sandals. She ran a comb through her short auburn curls, refreshed her lipstick, and sprayed on a touch of perfume before she headed for the door.

Her husband was relaxing on the couch, watching a basketball game. John looked quizzically at Valerie as she opened the back door. "Where are you going in such a hurry?" he asked.

Valerie chose a couple of magazines from the coffee table and tried to appear casual. She'd forgotten that John had Saturday off this week.

"Oh, I'm just going to the park for a couple of hours," she said airily.

If John sensed that something was amiss, he didn't let on.

"Well, don't forget that we have the farewell dinner for the missionary couple tonight at church."

"I'll be back in time," she said over her shoulder as she slipped out the door.

I hope I haven't missed him, Valerie thought, walking more quickly than usual. She resented her husband's inquiry about her activities. After all, if she wanted to have a little time to spend her way before she played her public role as the contented wife, that was her business.

Valerie arrived at the park, scrambled off the path she had begun to follow, and skirted a small hill to get to her bench faster. Descending the hill she stopped, frozen by what she saw in front of her. A mother with two small children was sitting on her bench. She was holding one baby on her lap and talking to the other child who was in a stroller.

Valerie winced, the way she had almost every time she'd seen young children lately. Her hand flew involuntarily to her stomach, and she remembered the pain of her childlessness yet again.

Then she started to pray. Maybe it was nothing—or maybe that woman was sitting on her bench as a test of her faith. In any case, it was an intrusion—and it was wasting more time she could have been spending with Curtis.

"Come on God, make her move," she whispered. "Make her move, please." Suddenly, the woman placed the baby on her lap back into the stroller, settled her other child, and pushed the stroller back onto the path and down the hill.

Valerie dashed to the bench before anyone else spied it, sat down, and mused over how quickly God had moved in response to her need. Surely He wouldn't have provided a place for her to meet Curtis if he disapproved of their friendship, would He?

Valerie waited and busied herself thumbing through the magazines she had brought. An hour passed, and no Curtis. She read some more and checked her watch again. Almost thirty minutes more had gone by. In another thirty minutes she would have to leave to dress for the dinner.

"Where can he be?" Valerie said to herself. She twisted her wedding ring around and around on her finger nervously, gazing at the one-carat solitaire. It was set in a wide gold nugget band that snuggled against a matching nugget band to form a pair. The diamond glittered and winked at her as if teasing her, taunting her. Valerie felt trapped, caught by John's ring that seemed to twinkle at her: "Gotcha!"

She sighed and chose another magazine from the pile she'd brought. Of course Curtis would have noticed her wedding rings. How could he have missed them? That must have been why Curtis didn't come. How could he have known that she only wore them as part of the charade she and John called a marriage? He couldn't have known that she hadn't really wanted to wear her rings for some time.

Valerie figured she might as well go home. Apparently Curtis was not going to show. Dejected, she gathered her things.

"Nice bench you've chosen out here under the trees," Curtis said, walking up just as she stood to leave. "Mind if I join you?"

"Sure," Valerie said, making room for Curtis on the small park bench. "Have a seat. Where's your guitar?" she asked, noticing that he'd come empty-handed.

"It's already at the church. I see you're still catching up on your reading."

"I am," she said. "I love to read. It relaxes me."

His eyes bore into her, and Valerie could tell he was curious about something. "Do you live near here?"

She nodded. "Do you know where Sierra Sand is?"

He seemed impressed. "That's a really nice subdivision," he said. "A nice neighborhood." He paused, letting his eyes drift slowly over her nut-brown skin and sparkling brown eyes. "Which brings me to another question."

"What's that?" she asked, blushing slightly under his perusal.

He nodded toward her left hand. "Where is your husband?"

"Right now he's at home, watching some game," she said, rolling her eyes.

"I can tell just looking at the rings on your finger that he cares a great deal about you," he said, raising an eyebrow. "I'm surprised he's not enjoying this fantastic day with his attractive . . . and mysterious wife."

"Th-Thank you for your compliment," Valerie stammered, ecstatic that Curtis thought she was attractive. "But, you're mistaken. I'm not at all mysterious. I just have some problems I need to think through."

Curtis seemed intrigued. "Maybe I can help you with your thinking." He placed his arm on the bench behind her, letting it graze her shoulder for a moment. "Do you have time to talk now?"

"Oh," she said, voice heavy with disappointment. "My husband and I are going to a dinner tonight, so I have to rush home today."

"That's too bad. I was going to invite you for a quick bite to eat before my rehearsal. Well . . . maybe next time."

"That would be great."

"Then you can tell me all about yourself, and about what's troubling you . . ." He paused and added, "And why you're not home with your husband." He took her hand, helping her to stand. "You had better get going." He squeezed her hand lightly. "See you next week around five."

Valerie floated all the way home.

TWO

JUST A FRIEND?

If the will of one person could have made the days of the week progress, Valerie would have made them move so that she wouldn't have to wait to see Curtis.

At one moment she was on cloud nine—daydreaming about the upcoming Saturday. At the very next moment she was in the deepest doldrums.

You fool, he won't come, she mused to herself on Wednesday as she poured a cup of coffee and made her way over to her desk. Here she was at work, with plenty to do to arrange an upcoming exhibit, but her thoughts kept drifting to Curtis.

Valerie didn't dare confide in anyone. She thought of telling two of her close friends at work but felt too uneasy. For one thing, they might think she was just reading things into a few innocent meetings. Besides, telling them about Curtis would mean revealing just how bad, how boring, things had become between John and her. She glanced at her shelf, where a photo of her husband smiled down on her. In the shot, his muscular arm was draped around her shoulder as they smiled for the camera. *Those were happier days,* she thought. *Before the infertility treatments, before the miscarriage, before my husband forgot how to meet my needs, before we started bickering so much.*

In any case, they looked like the perfect couple in that photo, and Valerie wasn't about to tell her coworkers that they weren't.

❋ ❋ ❋

Valerie frowned, annoyed to see her husband parked in front of the television yet again. It was Saturday, and apparently John didn't have to work. Well, she hoped he wouldn't interfere with her weekend plans. After all, she had a five o'clock date to keep.

Valerie blushed. Was she really thinking of their get-together as a date?

John noticed her bustling around the house, hurrying to finish her work again. "Valerie, are you going somewhere?" he asked.

"Just to the park," she said. "I want to do some reading, and the noise is distracting to me."

John seemed annoyed. "Did you forget that we're supposed to visit my Mom today for her birthday?"

Valerie met his irritation with her own. "I'm not going to be able to go, John. I've got a big meeting with several of the museum's key donors on Monday, and you know how tired that long drive to your mother's makes me. I've got to be at my best on Monday, and that won't happen if I've been stuck in the car for most of today and tomorrow."

She plucked a gift bag from the corner of the room and set it on the coffee table.

"Here's a gift for her. Tell her I said hello," she said indifferently.

John looked at Valerie with a strange expression in his eyes. Whether it was disbelief or disappointment, she couldn't tell. It didn't matter, though, because she didn't care. John never considered her plans or her schedule, or whether she'd even wanted to visit his mother. He never thought about her feelings or interests at all. He could go by himself.

She didn't plan on missing her time with Curtis. She'd been looking forward to it all week.

Valerie had only been waiting for about fifteen minutes when Curtis strode into view.

"Hey, pretty lady," he said, handing her a daisy he'd plucked along the path. Valerie marveled at his attentiveness. How long had it been since John had brought her flowers? She twirled the daisy between her fingers.

"Are you hungry? I'd like to treat my new friend to a late lunch, if you don't mind," he asked flirtatiously.

"Why thank you, kind sir," she said.

"I know just the place," he said, gesturing toward the food court at a nearby mall.

Valerie smiled up at Curtis as they walked toward the mall. It seemed perfectly innocent to her. After all, they were going to be eating out in the open. Curtis was, like he'd said, a new friend. They had nothing to hide.

❊ ❊ ❊

"He just assumed that you'd want to ride with him? Didn't he bother to ask what you wanted?" Curtis asked incredulously.

Valerie nodded, feeling justified in her anger. "And that's how it's been for the last couple of years. John is so inconsiderate! And when I needed him the most—when I was really hurting after my miscarriage—he bailed on me. He never seemed to understand how I felt, never seemed interested when I wanted to talk. Sometimes I don't think he cares about me at all, Curtis," Valerie said, poking at what was left of a club sandwich. "I feel trapped in my marriage."

Curtis nodded, his eyes sympathetic. He commiserated with Valerie, he told her. He'd been married before, several years ago. His ex-wife and son lived in another state.

Valerie was surprised. She couldn't imagine anyone divorcing the man sitting across from her. He'd listened to her sound off about her marriage for more than an hour, his face shadowed with concern. It was evident that he felt her pain, and she felt completely justified in opening up to him. After all, Valerie reasoned, she wasn't being unfaithful to John by having a simple lunch with Curtis. In fact, John should have been grateful to her for remaining in a marriage that had failed so miserably.

The shades of dusk stealthily taking over the sky seemed to fuel their desire to talk. Valerie realized that she needed to get home, and Curtis had a rehearsal to go to. As they walked back to the park, Curtis gently took Valerie's hand in his. Soon they were standing in front of their bench, each groping for words that would say goodnight, yet not good-bye. They blurted out their words at the same time.

"You go first," he chuckled, still holding her hand.

"I was going to say I have really enjoyed talking with you —being with you," Valerie said shyly.

"And I with you. Let's do it again next week, only some-place a little more . . . " He paused, choosing his word care-fully. "Intimate." He gently squeezed her hand, then walked away in the direction of his church.

On the walk home Valerie thought about John and how he would feel if he knew how happy she was. Then she rea-soned, *Why be concerned with him? He was the reason I'd gone to that park in the first place.*

❋ ❋ ❋

John wasn't home when his wife slipped out the front door the next Saturday for her meeting with Curtis. Other-wise he might have noticed how nicely she was dressed to go and sit on a park bench. She did not wear sneakers or jeans or even a warm-up. Instead, her sandals matched her rose silk pantsuit perfectly.

John might also have noted that Valerie had not dressed this carefully for him in months. Although she always looked very good when they attended church or some other function, she'd taken to wearing worn jeans and sweatshirts around the house. Valerie wasn't interested in being intimate with John anymore and hadn't been for some time, so she didn't bother to dress nicely around the house.

Shaded by the thick branches of the massive tree that hung low over her favorite bench, Valerie waited for Curtis, wondering where their innocent tête-à-tête might be headed. Could she continue with what held the promise of becoming a lengthy friendship . . . or more?

I'm not doing anything wrong. It's just an innocent meeting. Besides, God would not let anything happen between Curtis and me until He's set me free from John, would He?

Valerie felt a twinge of emotion and ran a gentle finger along her bottom lash to wipe away a tear that had formed at the thought of leaving John. What was happening to her? And what was she feeling? Remorse? Guilt? Love? For John? She shook her head, banishing the thought.

It was probably just a little fear about leaving her "comfort zone." And as unpleasant as it had become, being with John was comfortable—familiar, anyway. *The deeper the rut, the more comfortable it is, if that's where you live,* she told herself. She was accustomed to living in the rut her marriage had fallen into. But when she looked out beyond that rut, she longed to be free.

Curtis stood in front of Valerie, interrupting her thoughts. Valerie felt a rush of warmth as her eyes met his.

"I didn't hear you come up," she said.

"You were deep in thought," he said, his warm voice soothing. "I didn't want to disturb you."

"Actually, I was . . . thinking of you," she admitted, surprised at her boldness. Was she flirting with him?

If she was, Curtis seemed more than ready to mirror her light mood. "I'll pay more than a penny for those thoughts," he said, raising an eyebrow suggestively.

"You should. They are certainly worth a lot more. Maybe I'll tell you later."

"I'll definitely be around to talk, whenever you're ready," he said confidentially, taking Valerie's hand to help her stand. "You look really great."

"I feel great, now," Valerie replied, basking in the glow of their banter. It was so much fun to talk to someone this way. "Now that you're here."

Arms linked for a time, they walked slowly toward his car. "We're riding? Where is this restaurant?"

"Not far, actually, but I thought it would be less conspicuous if I drove."

On the short drive over to the Mexican restaurant Curtis voiced his concern about Valerie's circumstances. "It is unfortunate, but sometimes I believe we marry the wrong person, and when the right one comes along we know it instantly."

"It is as if you can feel something inside of you drawing you to that other person," she agreed, emphatically.

"Exactly. I believe God gives us that as the way for us to make the most suitable match."

They continued their conversation over dinner. Valerie ignored the warning bells inside her head that continuously clanged the words, *You are playing with fire.* She did not want to hear it. She had not done anything wrong, and she didn't plan on it.

"You see, it sounds to me like you and your husband are . . . here," Curtis said, stretching his arms apart to indicate the distance between his hands. "But maybe, just maybe, God still has someone for you who you could share real closeness with," he said, bringing his hands together and locking his fingers. "Like this." He leaned forward. "Valerie, maybe I'm that person," he said smoothly. "Think about it. I care about you, and I think we could have something special together. You just said John doesn't care about you, and I'm tired of feeling like we're sneaking around when I meet with you. It's only been a few weeks, but I already know that I'd like our friendship to move forward." He paused. "I'd never make you feel unappreciated the way John does."

The pastor of the Townsends' church walked over just as Curtis finished his sentence.

"Hello," Valerie sputtered, struggling to regain her composure after Curtis' declaration and the shock of seeing her pastor. Determined not to appear flustered, she introduced Curtis to Rev. and Mrs. Collins. Fortunately, Curtis had heard of Rev. Collins and knew a little about him, so the brief conversation they held flowed smoothly. Valerie explained that John could not make it, and promised to take him their regards.

But the spell was broken. The moment was gone, and recapturing it was not possible. Curtis looked at her with a tiny smile at the corners of his mouth. "You worried?"

"No," Valerie lied.

She was plenty worried. Pastor Collins might innocently mention to John that he had seen her with Curtis. So she decided to beat him to the punch. She would tell John that she had seen Pastor Collins.

When Valerie walked into the house, John was sitting in the living room watching television. She immediately began her story. Her back to him so that he could not see her face, she told him that she had decided to go to the Mexican restaurant a few blocks from the park, and had run into Rev. and Mrs. Collins.

"I wondered where you were," John said, missing the panicked look that flashed across her face. "You didn't answer your cell phone when I called, so I went to the park to see if you wanted to go to a fish fry at Paul and Sandra's."

"Is there still time to make it?" Valerie asked, cautiously.

"Yeah, but you've already eaten," he replied, an edge in his voice.

"We can still go," Valerie said, trying to insert a note of lightness into her voice. "I'll be ready in a minute."

Three

A CLOSE CALL

John and Valerie are here!" Sandra yelled over her shoulder as she met them at the front door. The crowd of familiar friends absorbed them on their way to the main room.

Valerie hugged her friend Janice and was startled to look directly into the eyes of Curtis Chambers. Her heart froze. He was observing her promenade through the throng with a look of amused pleasure.

His nod deliberately slow, with just a hint of a smile more visible in his eyes than on his lips, Curtis acknowledged her. No one appeared to have seen their exchange.

Curtis was with a group of five men in the center of the room on a raised platform. They were preparing to perform. "I didn't know there would be live entertainment," Valerie commented to Janice.

"Paul and Sandra always have great music," she replied.

"Sure," added Charlotte, another friend. "This time it's this fantastic new local Christian band, Praise. Sometimes they have well-known artists. Remember the group from a couple of years ago?"

Curtis had mentioned that his band was scheduled to play that evening, but had Valerie known where, she would never have insisted on coming. The six-member band began to play and sing, and the crowd became an audience.

When Curtis stepped up to the center microphone to sing lead, Valerie's dismay came full circle. He sang: "Wait on the Lord, you'll make the right choice."

Is he singing to me? Valerie wondered.

As she was standing there listening, Frank Partee, one of the few church members Valerie disliked, came and stood next to her. He spoke, commenting on how good the band sounded, then lowered the boom: "Saw you in the park today. You go there often?"

Valerie sensed that Frank was trying to back her into a corner somehow, and responded defiantly. "Not often," she said, looking directly into his eyes. "Only when I want to be alone and do some reading," she said.

"Oh? Is that what you do?" he replied, sarcastically. Did he cut his shifty eyes toward the band? She couldn't tell. Maybe Frank was trying to rub her face in something. Or maybe he was just his usual, irritating self.

Frank's comments made Valerie pause, though. If Frank had seen her with Curtis, that could have been disastrous. Her heart was pounding furiously at the prospect of having been found out.

Her eyes searched the room for John. She was ready to feign a headache, ready to make some excuse so they could leave. But he was caught up in conversation with one of the church deacons, balancing a plate in one hand and a plastic cup in the other. To calm down, she wandered outside onto the brick patio. Janice, Charlotte, and some more friends were seated in the breakfast area talking.

Valerie made a mental note to join them once back inside. But right then, she needed to clear her head. There were many questions she needed to answer. Feelings she had to sort through and figure out.

Valerie sighed as she stepped onto the patio, letting the cool breeze caress her face. What was she going to do about

Curtis? Her desire for him—she had to admit to herself that's what it was—had progressed from a simmer to a boil, and she struggled to contain it. After all, she didn't plan to break her marriage vows. Or had she already broken them by forming such an intense emotional attachment to a man who was not her husband? Or was it God's way of letting her out of her loveless marriage? After all, she hadn't been looking for Curtis, so God must have placed him in her life, she mused.

Standing there on the moonlit patio with the gentle summer breeze blowing feather-light against her face and arms, Valerie began to think back about John. Memories of having a burning desire for him like she thought she had for Curtis flooded her mind. They'd had some good times. In the beginning—and for the first few years of their marriage—they'd been passionate about each other. But was she the same person she'd been? Was John? Did their marriage stand a chance, after the long, alternating periods of silence and arguments?

Just then, she felt a soft whisper at her ear. "I'll give you a whole dollar for your thoughts." Valerie jumped, startled out of her reverie by the gentle pressure of Curtis' hand on her elbow.

He laughed softly. "Don't run. I just came out to say hello."

She hadn't heard the band stop. Valerie flushed as she realized that she and Curtis were standing alone on a moonlit-drenched patio, just a few yards from her husband. She inched backward toward the door.

Curtis smiled. "Don't worry, Valerie. You don't have to answer the question I asked you just yet. I can give you time to think about it. See you Saturday," he whispered. He moved toward her and slipped a loose tendril of her hair back into place.

Valerie hadn't seen John's shadow looming over the patio until she'd started to back away from Curtis. When she turned to step into the house, John was standing in the doorway. She wasn't sure how much he'd seen or heard. Curtis hadn't seemed to notice his presence either, so Valerie hoped he'd just gotten there.

"Oh, here's John," Valerie said with a false lightness, trying to cover her embarrassment. "I didn't see you standing there," she said, avoiding his eyes. "Were you looking for me?"

"As a matter of fact, I was," John said, eyeing her warily as he stepped onto the patio. "Janice and some of the other ladies want to see you inside. Before you go, why don't you introduce me to your friend?" His manner was pleasant enough, she thought.

"Sure. John, this is Curtis Chambers." Before she could say anymore, John took over. He obviously had come onto the patio to find out Valerie's connection with Curtis.

"I don't believe I have ever met you," he said, acknowledging Curtis icily.

"No, I don't think we have ever met. I know a few people from your church, though."

"Like my wife . . ." The thin smile accompanying John's words revealed his true feelings. Valerie was stunned. Had she been found out? How could she explain her actions to her husband?

Curtis answered, "Your wife, the Simons . . . uh . . .Tom and Judy Johnson, the sportscaster Leon Howard. Of course, I know Paul and Sandra." When he said the last names he gestured with his hand to include the whole house. "Now that I think about it, I know quite a few people here."

John said, "Yeah, you do. There is something I want to talk with you about. Something I just noticed. It appears from standing inside observing you walk out here, that you have more than a passing interest—." He stopped mid-sentence and motioned with his head toward the house.

"You're needed inside," he told Valerie sharply. "Curtis—" he spat out the name like a swear word—"and I can take it from here." She nodded and disappeared into the house to join her friends, who were discussing a statewide ladies' re-

treat coming to the area in two weeks. They all decided to go
and share hotel rooms. Most of the group had already discussed it with their husbands, and they wondered if Valerie
needed to talk with John before reserving a space at the hotel.

"Of course, I'd love to go," she said, hoping she sounded
more composed than she felt. "Let me talk to John about it."
She could get only a glimpse of the two men on the patio.
They continued to stand near the door, talking. After a few
minutes John came inside, then Curtis strode back to the
center of the room as the band prepared to play another set.

Valerie found John talking with Paul and Frank Partee.
Disregarding the satisfied expression on Frank's face, she
walked over to her husband.

"John, do you have a moment?" she said, more pleasantly
than she felt. "I want to ask you about the women's conference coming to town in a few weeks."

"Excuse me," John nodded, stepping away from his
friends. He placed his arm around her waist, and they
walked a short distance from the two men. Caught off-guard
by John's action, Valerie stumbled and leaned against him,
which made them look as though they could not keep their
hands off of each other.

But they both knew that nothing was farther from the
truth.

What had caused this unexpected display of affection? Valerie
wondered.

*What had been said on the patio? Does John feel threatened? Or is he
just maintaining the charade for the people who are watching?*

"John, Janice and some of the other women from church
are planning to attend a retreat in a few weeks," Valerie said.
"I need to let them know whether or not I can reserve a
room. I'd like to go," she added.

John hadn't been interested in the details of her comings
and goings for some time. But today, he seemed to want a lot
of information about the conference: who was sponsoring it,
where it would be held, what the dates were, even what the

theme was. When Valerie had satisfied him with her answers, he agreed that it would be good for her to go.

On the drive home, John was tight-lipped. He said nothing about his conversation with Curtis. However, when he
turned into the driveway, he turned to Valerie. "I don't know
what's going on with you and Curtis," he said, looking directly at her, "but I don't like the way it looks."

She opened her mouth to tell him that nothing had happened between her and Curtis. She began to protest that she
and Curtis were merely friends. But, once in the garage, John
cut her off as he got out of the car. "I have discussed this as
much as I want to tonight, Valerie. Goodnight." He walked
into the house and into his bedroom. She was left standing
in the garage, alone.

✻ ✻ ✻

At home that night, Valerie detected what she thought
were signs of John wanting to come into the master bedroom, instead of sleeping in the guest room as he normally
did. They hadn't been intimate in months, and John had
moved out of their bedroom months before that. After he
had showered and gotten ready for bed, he lingered in the
family room, and she saw his eyes follow her when she
walked toward the bedroom.

His actions gave her plenty to think about once she was
on the other side of the door. Valerie lay awake reliving the
ups and downs of the day. She winced as she thought about
how many lies she'd told in just a few hours. Valerie was not
accustomed to openly lying. But since she'd started seeing
Curtis, she felt like she'd been telling everyone a series of
half-truths. She was used to playing the role of the doting
wife. She wasn't used to telling outright lies. And she definitely wasn't used to almost being caught.

Four

A Change of Heart

When the day of the retreat came, Valerie packed a small bag, her Bible and journal, and got reluctantly into the car. It was Friday evening, and she was tired. She didn't really feel like missing a weekend when she'd see Curtis. And she wasn't really in the mood to be at a retreat, either. She'd been to several women's retreats over the past few years, and she didn't expect to learn anything new.

As she drove to the hotel where the three-day retreat would be held, Valerie found herself wondering how easy it would be to find Curtis and spend the weekend at a hotel with him instead. *After all, it wasn't like anything wrong would happen*, Valerie reasoned. *They were both Christians. Surely they'd be able to restrain themselves.* She fingered her cell phone absently, wondering if she should give him a call.

Her thoughts were interrupted as she turned into the hotel parking lot. Janice had already arrived and was waving her over so they could walk in together. Valerie saw her friend's enthusiasm but still couldn't work up any of her own. This was just not how she wanted to spend her weekend.

She confessed her poor attitude to Janice as they headed toward the registration table.

"Honestly, Janice, I just don't know if I'll hear anything fresh," she grumbled. "I'm not sure if I wouldn't be better off just sleeping or doing housework this weekend."

Janice placed an arm around her friend. "Oh, Valerie, just think of it as a good time to give yourself a spiritual checkup, if nothing else," she said, giving her a gentle squeeze. "Even if you don't hear something new, you can always think about whether or not you're living the truths you already know."

Janice, whose attractive salt-and-pepper hair was the only indication that she was in her mid-fifties, had befriended Valerie since she and John had joined their church. Valerie always appreciated the older woman's advice on other matters, so she promised herself that she'd try to have a good attitude about the retreat too.

There were several parts of the conference that Valerie found familiar. Nationally known conference speakers encouraged attendees with advice that ranged from personal care and pampering suggestions to tips for forming prayer support groups. Plenary speakers spoke on topics like active submission, or a woman's choice to defer to her husband, and the importance of being genuine in their relationships with their husbands and close friends.

Still, there were two elements that truly spoke to Valerie's needs.

One of the general sessions was a forum called "Express Yourself." Women were invited to ask questions about difficulties on their jobs, at their churches, and in their homes. A Christian psychologist would respond, and then a woman on a special prayer panel would take the woman aside for prayer.

Valerie wanted to confide in someone to help her think through Curtis' question. She even wanted someone to pray with her about whether or not she should leave her unfulfilling marriage. But she didn't want to speak about something so personal in front of so many women she knew. Disappointed, she felt the weight of her situation more heavily.

In another session, the leader instructed each woman to
pair up with another for special prayer. A woman who introduced herself as Patricia tapped Valerie's shoulder gently and
asked if she wanted to pray about any personal struggles or
challenges.

Valerie couldn't wait any longer. As Patricia took her
hand, she blurted, "I'm thinking about leaving my husband."
She felt strange sharing her struggle with a stranger, but at
the same time, she was comforted by the fact that she probably wouldn't see Patricia again.

Valerie explained her situation in detail: How happy she
had been before, their struggle with infertility, the pain of
her miscarriage, the way her relationship with John had
grown cold. She even shared how John had left their bedroom for the guest room and told Patricia how her friendship
with Curtis was quickly becoming more than she could
manage.

"If I have to remain in this marriage much longer, my
spirit is going to wither and die," she blurted. "Every time I
think that I might have to stay in it, I get depressed." Valerie
admitted to Patricia that she had prayed to be released, so
that she could find a relationship that gave her all the things
she felt her marriage lacked—love, trust, caring, conversation, and understanding.

"I need to get entirely out of this marriage, and stop
living this lie," she said, tears slipping down her cheeks.

Patricia looked at her with concern in her eyes. "I'll be
happy to pray for you," she said gently. "It's clear that you are
hurting, but I know that God can make something good
even out of this struggle, I promise."

The two women bowed their heads, and Patricia began
to pray for Valerie.

"Dear heavenly Father, my sister is hurting. She needs to
glimpse Your will for her life. She believes that the breakup
of her marriage is Your will, Father. But, we know that You
hate divorce. So, Lord, we ask that You show us Your will.

We ask You, Lord, to direct and ultimately guide her into total obedience to Your will."

Valerie was stunned. This was not the prayer she'd wanted, not even close. She felt heat rising to her cheeks and tried to pull away, but Patricia gripped her hands tightly.

"As for Valerie's husband, Lord, work in his life as well. Cause him to become a man whom she can respect. Father, we realize that the path You have selected for her may not be easy, but we don't ask for the easy way out. I believe, Father, that You desire that she remain in her marriage. I believe that You have some splendid things to show her, that You have not disregarded her pleas, but instead are waiting on her to study Your word about divorce and marriage. We agree together that where You lead, she will follow. Teach her Lord, to take You into their life together and into their marriage bed. Fix it, Lord, so that she completely trusts You in this and all areas of her life. And Father, let her speak no more of leaving a union You honor. We pray this prayer in the name of Your precious Son, Jesus. Amen."

Valerie looked up when the prayer was over, certain her fury was reflected in her eyes. Here she had poured out her heart to a stranger who had approached her to pray, and this woman had completely disregarded her feelings. She felt betrayed.

If Patricia noticed how angry Valerie was, she didn't let on. Looking at her prayer partner with sadness in her eyes, she squeezed her hand gently. "God bless you, Valerie," she said softly. "God bless you and your marriage."

Valerie refused to feel changed by the prayer. As a matter of fact, she felt even more decisive about leaving John. After all, hadn't God provided a caring man who found her attractive and complimented her? Wouldn't He be willing to give her a second chance at marriage, a second chance to get things right, with the right man this time?

Valerie was still angry and flustered when the sessions broke for dinner that evening, and Janice noticed.

"Valerie, what's wrong?" Janice asked, cocking her head to one side. "The way you're attacking that salad, you'd think it did something to you," she said, making a light attempt at humor.

Valerie was not amused. "I shared some very personal things with my prayer partner in that last session," she said, "but she didn't pray the way I'd wanted her to at all."

Because they were sitting alone, Janice asked Valerie what issues she was facing that made her so upset.

"I've been very unhappy in my marriage for some time now," Valerie confessed. "I've met a man, a kind man named Curtis, who has asked me to think about leaving John for him, and—" she paused, not sure if she really wanted to share as much as she had, then plunged ahead. "And I'm really thinking about it, Janice."

To Valerie's surprise, Janice didn't seem shocked or outraged at her news. Instead, she nodded gently. "Marriage can be very difficult sometimes," she said, sympathy in her tone. "I can remember several years that were rough for Tim and me, and there were plenty of times I wanted to give up," she said.

Valerie shook her head, not understanding. Tim and Janice were often teased for being one of the more affectionate couples at the church. She couldn't imagine them ever being close to divorcing. Then again, few people could imagine the nature of the false front she and John maintained.

"Val, I'm your friend, and I'm not going to lecture you," Janice said. "But I will pray that you do what you know is right," she said, looking deep into her friend's eyes. "And because I care about you, I'm going to ask you every so often if you're making your best effort to build a strong marriage," she said.

Valerie shrugged and looked away. She wasn't sure what she wanted, but she knew she didn't want her marriage to stay the way it was.

❋ ❋ ❋

Although the "Express Yourself" session and the prayer time with Patricia did little to soften her heart, the final session she attended spoke to her very core. She looked up as the speaker was introduced and was startled when she realized that it was her prayer partner, Patricia!

In the session, titled "Wait on the Lord," Patricia challenged the women to rethink the meaning of the term "wait." Valerie copied Patricia's quotation down in her journal: "To wait is not to sit back, expecting God to provide an automatic solution to your problems. Waiting is preparing yourself by remaining in God's will so you will be ready to act when He intervenes."

"You see, sometimes, when we really want a change in our lives, we move ourselves instead of waiting for God's solution," Patricia said, walking back and forth on the podium. "We fantasize and strategize, trying to bring about something that we know is not God's will for our lives."

For the first time since she'd come to the conference, Valerie felt deeply convicted. Patricia was right. For several weeks now she'd been living a fantasy instead of thinking about what she needed to change in herself to improve her marriage.

She admitted that in her mind, she'd been thinking of Curtis as God's solution to her problem. She wanted so badly to be rid of her marriage, she had cast him in the role of rescuer. She'd begun to direct her own play. She realized that she'd been writing the last scenes of her marriage, pretending that God would approve.

Valerie stared at the quotation she'd written down. She wasn't completely sure she was supposed to stay married to John. But she knew she would have to let go of Curtis.

Five

Truth and
Consequences

The next Saturday was warm and sunny. But Valerie felt none of the exuberance she usually felt when she thought about going to meet Curtis.

She knew what she had to do, but she wasn't sure if she wanted to do it. Apprehensive and saddled with guilt, Valerie trudged to the park and sat nervously on her bench, wondering if Curtis would come. After all, she had missed the Saturday they'd intended to meet after the party.

Wouldn't it be nice if God got me out of this by causing him to perceive my no-show as a rejection? She wondered. That would make getting right with God that much easier for her. Maybe God was using the weather to end the relationship without Valerie saying a word. It had rained the weekend they had planned to meet. The next weekend she was away at the retreat. It would be so much easier to break off her affair with Curtis just by failing to show up for a few weeks.

Her *affair* with Curtis. The term sounded so illicit. But she'd come to believe that that was exactly what had developed between them. And during the week since the retreat, she'd decided that if she really wanted to give God a chance to work in her marriage, she had to be honest with herself.

I can't blame anyone else for this situation. This is my fault, Valerie thought, gripping the seat of the park bench and staring into the grass in front of her. *I've been having an affair with Curtis.*

She lowered her head, feeling again the wave of shame that had swept over her when she'd admitted it to herself.

No, we haven't been physically intimate, but I've been emotionally intimate with him, she thought. *I've been giving him the parts of my heart, the parts of my soul that should belong to my husband. It's true that my marriage is far from perfect. But I feel guilty. I've been dreaming about Curtis instead of deciding whether or not I really wanted to fix things with John. Instead of talking to my husband about our problems, I shared them with another man. If I'm not strong enough to break this off today, there's no way I can really pretend it's God's will.*

Valerie wondered nervously if she'd remember the words she'd planned to say. She'd practiced all week—in the car on the way to work, in front of the mirror before bed, in the shower. Now, though, only brief phrases flew through her mind. And how would she begin? Valerie tested different phrases, her tentativeness reflected in her voice.

"I lost my mind," she ventured softly, hoping no one heard her as she sat there. "I don't know what came over me." "I'm embarrassed by my actions." All seemed like good places to begin. Agonizing over every detail, she wondered how Curtis would respond. What would he say? Would his facial expression change, would those gorgeous grey-green eyes cloud with pain?

Maybe he won't care at all, she thought, surprised at the twinge of pain she felt at the thought. *Maybe he'll laugh in my face and insist there had been nothing more to his actions than just befriending an unhappily married woman. Maybe he'd say we were only friends.*

The wait was long, and Valerie felt strangely conspicuous. Before, she'd felt sheltered sitting on her park bench. Now, she felt exposed.

Curtis strode jauntily toward their familiar spot, slid next to her on the bench seat, stretched his legs languorously in front of him and said, "Top of the evening to you." His usual cheery self, he affectionately accused her of toying with him by not showing up the previous Saturday. But Valerie was too tense for small talk. She took a deep breath.

"Curtis, I won't be coming here to see you anymore."

"Oh?" His pause was heavy — pregnant with questions she knew deserved answers.

Valerie stared across the plot of grass that separated them from a children's play area. Children were playing, screeching and squealing with delight as they ran and jumped and hung upside down, their legs wrapped around a wooden bar. Two small boys were sliding together down a slide. Once at the bottom, they would each scamper around opposite sides, racing to see who would get to the ladder and up the rungs first.

She concentrated on the two little boys and their place in the bigger picture of kids spinning round and round on the merry-go-round, chasing each other, zigzagging in circles, and sailing up and down on the seesaw. Their shrieks reverberated all over the park. The two little boys just kept sliding together, running around the slide and racing up the ladder to the top.

Valerie sighed, wondering if she'd ever experience that kind of innocent, infectious happiness again. If it hadn't been for one of those kids losing control of his ball on a Saturday not so long before, she and Curtis would never have met. There she was, ending things where they'd begun—in a park, amid the gaiety and naiveté of children.

"Has something changed?" Curtis' words jolted Valerie back to reality and the task at hand. She didn't know what to say, but she knew her answer would be critical. Her words could create such an intense feeling between them that neither of them could pretend their relationship was innocent. Or they could end her contact with Curtis once and for all.

She wanted to say that her every thought was of him, and that her guilt was consuming her. On the other hand, she knew, she could admit at the retreat she'd received a clearer perspective on what God expected of her in her marriage. And part of that insight was that Curtis couldn't be a part of her life before her marriage was over.

Valerie took a deep breath.

"Curtis, I attended a retreat last week."

"I know." He answered slowly, as though he already knew her next words. "I figured that's where you were."

"God showed me that to involve myself with you in any way while I am still married is not what He wants. I believe my marriage will end, but I want to be careful I don't do anything to slow the process."

His next words were a near murmur. "Seeing me, talking with me is slowing you down?"

She shook her head no.

"Then . . . could it be you were frightened by what happened the last time I saw you?" Curtis asked, squinting his eyes and shielding them from the sunlight.

"That could have something to do with it," Valerie conceded. "If we do end up together, I want to be open about us."

"Yet you want to stop seeing me."

"I have to," she said, trying to be patient. "I am still married."

"From what you've told me, in name only."

"I should not have told you that. You probably saw me as a desperate woman needing a man's attention."

"I saw you as a very attractive woman trapped in a marriage she never wanted, with a man who never knew how to treat her, or love her."

"Curtis, I don't know if that's true or not."

"You don't know what you want, do you?"

He reached out to stroke her face and seemed surprised when she jerked back, shaking her head.

"You want someone who can love you like you want to be loved," Curtis continued, the passion in his voice rising.

"You want"—he pulled his hands together the way he had that night in the restaurant —"this. Valerie, I know you do."

"Curtis, I don't know what I want," Valerie said, tears trickling down her face. "I don't know if I can fix my marriage, or if I even want to. I don't know if John wants to fix our marriage. I don't know if I want in or out."

Valerie paused and inhaled, calming herself.

"But I do know that it's not appropriate for us to be—like we are—while I'm married."

"So when you're not married"—Valerie heard the question in his voice and shook her head, cutting him off.

Curtis regained his composure and stood. He appeared hurt. Not devastated, just hurt. It was as if he had plans that included Valerie but would have to change them.

"Well, my pretty lady, I guess this is goodbye," he said, taking her hand to help her stand. He looked deep into her eyes. "You know you were getting to my heart, don't you?"

Valerie wanted to plead with Curtis to give her just a little more time—a couple of months, tops. She wanted so badly to say those words. But she could not.

But Curtis had something to say, something she never would have expected.

"I was going to ask you if you would consider moving out of state."

"What? Why out of state?"

"Because I'm leaving. My job has offered me a transfer and a promotion. I cannot pass it up."

Valerie was speechless. She felt so forlorn, so alone. She almost whimpered. Strangely, though she knew she had to end her relationship with Curtis, she wasn't really prepared for the possibility of never seeing him again. His leaving sealed the ending to what she'd secretly hoped would be an open-ended goodbye.

"I—I guess this is really goodbye," she stammered softly, trying not to show her shock.

Curtis touched Valerie's chin lightly with his thumb, lifting her face so that she looked directly into his eyes. Those gorgeous, gray-green eyes. "Yes, Valerie, this is really good-bye."

She knew he wanted to kiss her. There they were in a park, visible to anyone there. Their faces were now so close she could feel the gentle sweep of his breath on her lips and saw herself reflected in his eyes under the orange glow of the setting sun. She knew what would come next, but didn't want to stop it.

I can't believe myself, she thought. *How can I want him and not want him at the same time? How can I know that I'm supposed to go back to my marriage, but be so ready to let Curtis kiss me and make things even more complicated?*

Then, something confusing happened. Like a panther that relished in the capture of its prey instead of the kill, Curtis pulled Valerie closer for a moment, then released his hold on her. Clutching her shoulders in his hands, he kissed her forehead and whispered in her ear so softly that she wondered if she'd really heard him.

"Bye, Valerie."

Curtis turned and walked away without looking back, and Valerie stood watching him go. His whispered goodbye still haunting her, she stood watching in the direction he had taken, long after he was gone from view.

Six

STIRRING THE EMBERS

Although Valerie had broken things off with Curtis, she still felt like her marriage to John was nothing more than pretense. As far as anyone knew they were a happy, devoted couple, living in a home filled with love and intimacy. Nothing was farther from the truth.

But Valerie and John played their parts well. They continued to be seen together among their friends at church. As always, Valerie held John's hand or arm in public but loosened it when she sensed that no one was looking.

Since she'd broken things off with Curtis, Valerie had sometimes wanted to warm up to her husband. But after so many months of living as embittered roommates, neither of them really knew where to begin.

Once, she'd even jokingly flirted that she would bet he had forgotten how the master bedroom looked, since he hadn't been in it for such a long time. John didn't hear her comment as an invitation. To him, it seemed to confirm that he'd been banished from the room. He replied that she did not have to worry—he'd take her word for it.

So much for my attempt at reconciliation, Valerie thought. *I don't know why I even tried.*

One Sunday during the announcement segment of the
morning service, the men's softball team was recognized as
having won the All-City Softball Tournament. John, voted
the team's most valuable player, was called to the podium to
accept the team's trophy.

As John strode to the podium to receive the award,
Valerie felt the approving glances from her friends in the
congregation. Janice looked over and waved. Everyone
seemed to feel that Valerie should be proud of her husband.
But just then, she felt more. She felt startled at the sudden
surge of attraction she felt for her husband. Startled—and
confused.

Am I just feeling prideful? she wondered. *Basking in the attention
I'm getting as the devoted wife? Do I truly want to be with my husband
for himself—or for how good our relationship makes me look to others?
It's been so long since I felt like this about John . . .*

On the ride home, Valerie searched for the words to tell
John how proud she was of him. But she struggled to think of
a way to pierce the thick veil of silence between them before
they arrived home.

Still, it was worth a try. As they walked into the house,
Valerie touched her husband's arm lightly.

"That was a nice trophy your team received," she ventured. "I didn't realize you'd done so well this season."

He pulled away from her touch. "That's because you've
never been to any of the games," he said, his voice strained
with sarcasm.

"Well, you know how I am about sports," she said with a
gentle laugh, trying to bring some lightness to the interchange.

He laughed sardonically, as though he'd been waiting for
her to say those exact words.

"Yeah, I know," he said dryly. "*Music* is more your thing."

Caught off-guard, there was nothing she could say to re-
cover her composure. Cheeks flaming, Valerie walked stiffly
into her bedroom, feeling strangely exposed. She wondered

if John thought something had happened between Curtis and her. Valerie felt the urge to run into the living room and scream at him, "Nothing happened!" But she knew that wasn't completely true. She felt the sting of tears brushing against her eyelids as she thought about how sweet things had been when her marriage was a love affair. So many things were different. Somewhere along the way the marriage had taken a turn for the worse. Still, the brief awards ceremony had forced Valerie to face the question that had been stirring her heart and mind for months:

Could she still love John?

Seven

꧁꧂

AWAKENINGS

The bitter exchange that Sunday afternoon crippled Valerie's hopes for a reconciliation with John. She stung inside whenever she remembered his cutting remark, the way his face had become an ugly snarl as he looked at her. He'd clearly hated what he'd seen.

Still, part of her fought the guilt she felt. *Does he blame me for the condition of our marriage?* she wondered angrily as she drove home from work one evening. *I'm not perfect, but I'm hardly the villain here,* she thought.

Valerie was uneasy, confused . . . heartbroken. A swirl of conflicting emotions surfaced, often within minutes, leaving her feeling unsettled. Certain that John knew about her relationship with Curtis, she imagined John twisting and distorting what had happened between them and felt a wave of rage and pain. Her character undoubtedly suffered severely under his scrutiny, and she resented that. Then she remembered that even though she and Curtis hadn't been physically intimate, she was far from innocent. Then she fought a crushing guilt.

On the other hand, Valerie stewed with anger at herself for letting John get the better of her. Why should she care what he thought?

Still, she was embarrassed by her failed marriage. What if someone discovered that she'd been unfaithful to her husband? What if someone realized that her marriage was a lifeless shell?

Later that week, Valerie decided to attend the monthly ladies' meeting at her church. This was a monthly event and she expected that it would hold no surprises, so her decision to attend was less than enthusiastic. However, she usually attended, so she put on her church face and went to the meeting. Valerie wondered if the sadness she felt was a reaction to the loss of Curtis or her ambivalence toward John. In any case, she didn't want to be alone with her thoughts.

At one point Valerie had thought that being a divorce statistic was preferable to the life she was living. As she sat and listened at the ladies' meeting, she became less certain of that, and more convinced that closing the book on the story of her marriage was not going to be all that easy.

She was surprised again to see that Patricia Carter was the invited speaker. *How unusual to keep running into the same woman like this!* she thought.

Today Patricia was speaking on Women Who Pray. Patricia considered God to be her confidant, saying she consulted Him on everything.

I used to be like that, Valerie thought. *I used to read my Bible regularly. I was always reading a commentary or some other book to help me understand what I was reading. When did that change? My prayers were much better then, not empty and flat like now,* she mused. *They seemed to have much more substance, and were a lot less repetitive.*

What had happened? When did I stop really praying? she wondered. *Well, I still pray,* she thought, feeling defensive. When it came to her marriage, she'd gone many times to God and told Him how a divorce would allow her and John to pursue the happiness they couldn't seem to find together. She'd spent hours explaining to God that her marriage was a failure, and that she'd be better off without her husband.

Valerie began to pay attention again, noticing that Patricia was writing on a whiteboard in the center of the room. "You see, we should always follow our prayers with action," Patricia said. "I want to give you some examples of prayer followed with action." Valerie picked up her pen and began to write down the examples Patricia was giving. And although Valerie was nodding her head in agreement with Patricia, she couldn't squelch a cynical thought:

Sure, I'll pray, but I expect God to act, not me.

Valerie lowered her head as she realized what she'd thought and asked God's forgiveness. Was that really how she felt? That everything was up to God, and she had no control over how she acted? No control over her part in the survival or failure of her marriage? She realized that she wasn't sure whether she should try to save her marriage, or whether she should leave John. She realized that she hadn't asked God about saving her marriage at all.

Her thoughts were interrupted again as Patricia pulled out a stopwatch.

"I'm not a very patient person at all. It's almost like I pray for what I want, and as soon as the prayer is over, I'm off my knees, looking at my stopwatch, clocking God's response time," she chuckled, shaking her head. The women in the group laughed with her. "I have to admit it," Patricia said. "Sometimes I want a 'stopwatch' God. And I know I'm not the only one." Patricia put her hands on her hips and pouted, mimicking a young child.

"Looooooord," she said, drawing out the name like a tattling child. "It's been fifteen minutes. When are you going to provide the money I need!" She paused. "Faaaaaather, I neeeeed a new job. I need it now!" Laughter filled the room as the ladies chuckled at Patricia's silliness—and saw how foolish they must have seemed to God at times. "Oooooh, you know my children just won't do right, and my marriage—" Patricia cut off her sentence, laughing at herself. "I need to close our meeting now, but let me leave you with something to think about," Patricia said, shaking her head as she recovered from her laughing fit. "When a woman opens her heart to God and has an honest straightforward talk with Him, something will change."

When the meeting was over, Valerie stopped by the church bookstore, where Patricia was autographing her latest book, *He's Changing Me*. As Patricia was signing Valerie's copy, she looked up and smiled. "How are you?" she said, clearly recognizing Valerie from the retreat. "I have been hoping I would run into you somewhere. I wanted to check and find out how things are going, Valerie. That is your name, isn't it?"

"Yes. I wondered if you remembered me."

"Not only do I remember you, you have been on my mind. I pray for you often." Other women had gotten in line to get an autograph and talk with her. She handed Valerie her book. "Can you wait here for a moment?" she asked.

Not sure what Patricia had in mind, Valerie waited as Patricia autographed a few more books. During a lull in the action, Patricia turned to her.

"I'd like to invite you to a Bible study I'm teaching."

Writing an address on the back of her card, she invited Valerie to attend along with Janice, who had walked up as they were speaking. As Valerie drove home, she marveled as she thought about Patricia praying for her and her marriage. She wondered how her marriage would look if she coupled prayer with action.

As she prepared for bed, she thought again about John.

Where did we go wrong? she wondered yet again. *When did we stop really living together and begin to have no more between us than just the same street address?*

Valerie felt a tear trickling down her face as she thought about the beginning of their marriage. It seemed so far away. Just seven years, but, she thought, they'd made them a long seven years by not caring enough to fight for their happiness. It was more than the sense that reality had settled in a few years after the glow of the honeymoon. It seemed like they'd run into problems, and, instead of really trying to work through them, Valerie and John had made an unspoken agreement to take the easy way out and fake a good marriage.

As she readied for bed, Valerie wondered if John was going to leave her soon. They'd left each other emotionally a couple of years ago, and leaving sexually had followed. Granted, he'd never said anything about leaving. Was he content to simply continue the deception? If he left that night, would Valerie care? Her head answered no. But a small, warm corner in her heart whispered yes.

As memories of a happier time flooded Valerie's mind, her eyes brimmed over and tears slid slowly down her face. Why had she spent all this time rejecting John?

She had reasoned that her husband was cruel, and that her rejection of his physical needs would force him to learn how she wanted to be treated. She'd smiled with satisfaction when her actions had, in effect, told him to get out of her face. That was her way of putting him in his place. Her form of payback. She'd even chosen to ignore her physical desire for John.

Let him know I don't need him, she'd thought. *Let him feel what it's like when someone's not at all interested in meeting your needs!*

Now, though, Valerie felt her heart telling her that their problems weren't only John's fault. He was the same man she'd married—and she'd known she wanted to marry him when he'd asked her. She'd had no doubts then. And when she was honest, she had to face that John wasn't cruel. Something—time, their struggle with infertility, something— had changed both of them.

She heard the garage door open and close, and the jingling of her husband's keys. John was home. He came inside, closed and locked the door. Then Valerie heard a moment's hesitation. It was as though John was deciding which door to choose—the one where she was, or his bedroom on the other side of the house. He moved. The door to the second bedroom closed shut. She began to cry softly again. After a few minutes, it opened and Valerie held her breath, hoping to see him standing in the doorway. Instead, she heard the sound of water from the shower in the guest bathroom.

John's actions were normal for them. It was Valerie's thinking that had changed. She was hurt. Hurt about everything. Sick and tired of the life she was living. But something kept tugging at her, insisting that she not give up, even though she wanted nothing more than to give up for good. Valerie wanted to be happy for a change. Again, she found herself fighting between hoping that her marriage could survive and despairing that it was already over. Already dead.

She brushed away the tears that had rolled down her cheeks onto her pillow. Did Valerie still love John? How could that be, when her one thought for months had been to get away from him? Did she really care about him, or was her body simply missing the intimacy they had once shared?

If we have any love left, Valerie thought, *it's a pitiful, pathetic love in need of someone greater than me to salvage it.* She remembered what Patricia had said about opening up to God and allowing him to change difficult situations. *That's really my only option,* she thought to herself.

Valerie pulled herself out of her bed and bowed beside it, gripping her sheets in her fists and burying her head in them.

"God help," she gasped. That's all she could think to say. "God help. Help me, please. Help us, please." Valerie realized she was groping for God-reaching words, biblical words. Words that came with study and prayer and thought. Words that would make God change her circumstances sooner. Words she couldn't find, didn't have.

"God, what has happened to me?" she moaned. "I'm not close to you anymore. I don't even know how to address you." From deep inside she whispered a screamed, "Help me!"

Then the words poured out of her. "Oh, Father, things are really bad here. We're living under the same roof, but there's so much hatred. There's so much wrong. I know some of the blame is mine. I'm not without blame. But John is the man. He's supposed to change. He just doesn't care. He wants us to be a couple when we're around other people, particularly our church friends. But it's a lie. We don't live as husband and wife. We don't have a relationship. We don't have a marriage. Until we get into an argument I feel as though I am living with a stranger. It's then that I know him all too well. Lord, John doesn't know what I need and he doesn't care."

Valerie's shoulders heaved with sobs and she pounded her fists on the bed as she poured out her frustration. "And Lord, I'm starting—I think—to care about him again, but I don't know what he needs. I don't know how to start."

Then Valerie wondered: Even though she and John hadn't felt close to one another for some time, they'd continued to be physically intimate until a few months ago. What if she set aside her pride and went to his room?

Valerie paused, intrigued by the thought. Her tears slowly stopped as she rose from the bed and moved to the vanity table outside the bathroom. She looked in the mirror and wondered what John would see if he saw her then. Would he notice that she'd been crying? Would he see her tears as a sign of her remorse over the way she'd acted? Would he know that she wanted to find some way to change things between them for the better? Or would John think Valerie was trying to manipulate him with her show of emotion? She had to find out.

Valerie showered and chose a sheer negligee. Then, with a whispered prayer, she spritzed her body with perfume and walked across the house to John's bedroom.

❀   ❀   ❀

Valerie stood in the hallway outside of her husband's open door, letting the light emphasize how her sheer gown gently skimmed her curves.

John had just emerged from the guest bathroom in a
crisp pair of pajama pants. Valerie could smell her husband's
cologne and felt a twinge of anticipation as he turned back
the covers and slipped into bed. She moved toward the door
and leaned into it.

"Hi," she said simply.

John looked up at her, and she noticed a flash of something—appreciation? annoyance?—pass over his face as his
eyes took her in.

"Yes?" he said brusquely, a hint of suspicion in his voice.

Valerie felt embarrassed. This was not the reception she
had hoped for.

"I've come to sleep in bed with my husband," she said,
moving boldly toward the other side of his bed.

John looked at her indifferently. "Fine," he said, turning
his back to her and reaching over to turn off the lamp on his
night table.

She'd come too far to leave without further wounding
her pride, so she pulled back the covers and slid in beside
him.

Valerie said that she planned to sleep next to him, and
her words were literally true. To her deep disappointment,
John didn't touch her all night.

In the glow of a nightlight, Valerie stared at John's
smooth back and muscular shoulders. She thought about
touching him, but she was too timid to try.

Part of her wanted to start an argument. In Valeric's
mind, even that kind of attention would have been preferable to the stony silence that hung like a canopy over the
bed.

Tears of humiliation welled in Valerie's eyes as she turned
her back to John. If her husband noticed her sniffling, he did
not respond.

❋ ❋ ❋

That night beside her husband was a turning point for Valerie. Although she hadn't been too interested in saving her marriage before, she realized that she did love her husband, and that perhaps it wasn't too late for God to restore things between John and her. Surely, she could give Him a few months.

Something inside of her knew God had heard her prayers. Valerie knew He would answer. But during those weeks following her visit to his bedroom there was absolutely no change in John that she could see. She wondered what God wanted her to do. She shared her feelings with Janice when she called to make plans for going to Patricia's Bible study together. "It sounds like you want to know God's will for your marriage," Janice said.

Valerie was stunned by the simplicity yet completeness of those words. God's will. Janice was right. In her life, in this marriage, what did God want?

Since she'd begun to pray again regularly, Valerie realized that until just a few weeks earlier, her concern for her marriage, and life, was what she wanted. How she was affected was priority one.

In fact, she hadn't really considered the quality of her marriage important to God. She suspected that she'd probably felt it was none of His business.

Valerie began to admit to herself that she'd never really let Jesus be Lord of her life. She'd done all of the "right" things—attended church all of her life, accepted Christ as a teenager, been involved with church activities, married a Christian man. Yet she'd never allowed Christ to rule in her life. As she arrived at Patricia's house for the Bible study, she sensed a new determination in her heart. She was determined to learn how to yield to God.

Eight

A NEW DIRECTION

Patricia answered the door when Janice and Valerie arrived. "Ladies, I'm so glad you could make it," she said, giving each of them a quick squeeze as she motioned them inside. When all the ladies had come, she led them in prayer and went right into the study.

After the prayer, Patricia handed each of the women a slip of paper and a pencil.

"I'd like to begin our time together with a brief exercise," she said. "When I travel and speak, women often speak to me about the problems they are having in their marriages. So today, since we'll be discussing marriage, I'd like each of you to write down the deepest concern you have for your marriage."

Valerie was taken aback. She hadn't expected the Bible study to be about marriage. Was this God's way of answering her prayer?

She stared at the blank sheet of paper and sighed softly. Where was she supposed to begin? Many of the women in the room seemed to share Valerie's reaction, and Patricia noticed.

"Don't worry," she said gently. "You don't need to sign

your name on your sheet, so please write freely. By sharing our concerns, we'll be able to help one another, so please don't feel nervous." Reassured, Valerie scribbled "my husband and I are barely friends. We live like trapped roommates" on her paper just as Patricia rose to collect the sheets.

Patricia nodded slowly as she read over each of the responses. "I can see a pattern here, and it doesn't really surprise me, because I've seen a similar thread in a lot of the e-mails I've received." She looked up and smiled. "We all seem to struggle with how to adequately respect our husbands."

The women looked around sheepishly. No one had expected to have the same problem as the others. "Don't be embarrassed," Patricia said. "This is really a more common problem than you think. I think that many of us are being lured by the world into thinking in ways other than how God would have us think." She paused and passed a plate of cookies around the room.

"It really tears at my heart to see Christian couples buy into worldly philosophies about relationships," she said. "It leads to a lot of pain and confusion. You see, worldly thinking promotes immorality and condones any combination of sexual partners. Godly thinking doesn't. The world advocates denying sexual intimacy to your mate. The Lord does not."

When she made her second comparison, Valerie knew she was guilty. She'd been so self-centered, she wondered if John even wanted her anymore. His refusal to touch her the night she'd gone to his bedroom seemed proof that he was no longer interested. When things first began to change between John and Valerie—when she'd first started to deny him—he would fall asleep in the family room watching television without coming to bed. Eventually, he'd moved into the second bedroom, and Valerie hadn't tried to stop him.

At the time, she'd been glad John had decided to leave her alone. But when Patricia pointed out that this was worldly thinking, she felt stunned. It hadn't occurred to her that "punishing" John this way was a worldly tactic. She was determined to make things right somehow.

"Consider the barrage of sex scenes, immoral relationships, and coarse joking transmitted for your absorption via the airwaves," she continued, concern for the women in her voice. "I know you think you are too strong in the Lord to be influenced by these things. But we are all influenced by what we continually see and hear—and when we are lured into thinking the world's way, we become trapped." She paused and smiled. "I want to talk to you about the lure of the Lord."

"The first step in exploring the lure of the Lord involves getting the 'marriage hierarchy' straight," Patricia said. "First, you've got to make Jesus Lord of your life—and that includes your marriage. So many times we're willing to accept Jesus as our Savior, but we're not willing to let Him control our lives. Isn't it funny, how we like to try and think ahead of God. It makes things so nice and neat. God may have other plans. You must remember to let Him lead, and stop trying to run His business."

Valerie realized that she'd been learning about that through her prayers. It was true that she'd been trying to live in a way she approved of, without consulting God for his direction. Valerie loved God. Still, she was scared to be obedient. What would God want from her? It seemed so risky somehow, she mused. She preferred to be in control, but she had to admit that her determination to do things her way hadn't made things better. Far from it.

"You won't be able to fully enjoy the gifts of marriage and emotional and sexual intimacy without making Jesus the head of your marriage," Patricia said. "Without Jesus, you'll make a complete mess of it. You won't know how to treat each other, how to relate to each other, how to put the other person first. While you are fighting your internal wars, hating your marriage bed, and woefully neglecting each other, you are closing the door on Jesus."

Valerie knew Patricia was right. Even though John had

played a role in making their marriage what it was, she was responsible too. Neither of them had made Jesus head of their marriage.

"I'd like to share something else with you, something that won't come easily," Patricia continued. "You must learn to put your husband first. Learn to respect him, the way God has said you should."

Valerie scribbled "Respect John?" in her notes.

It's true that John and I have our differences—serious differences, she thought. *But would we be in the place where we are if we respected one another, or even if I'd respected him enough to share my concerns with him instead of just shutting down sexually—or turning to another man with my concerns? Lord, I'm seeing how much my poor choices have contributed to the breakdown of my marriage. I can't control John and his choices, but I can control myself with Your help.*

"With God," Patricia said, "there is no his side, her side. There is only one side, God's side. So we are going to examine just what is God's side." She directed the women to 1 Corinthians chapters 6 and 7, and together they discussed the end of 6 and all of 7.

"First, know that your body is a member of Christ. Let Him have charge over it," Patricia said, encouraging the women to make sure they did what Christ would want. "Remember, your bodies are the temple of the Holy Spirit. They are designed to glorify God, and that includes the way you act in your marriages. Don't forget that God has given your body to your husband and his body to you."

Patricia paused, then repeated herself for emphasis as Valerie scribbled in her notes. "I want to be very clear on this part of the Scripture," she said. "As far as God is concerned, when you marry, your body belongs to your husband. Indeed it is your husband's body. He has given the authority of his body to you, and authority over your body to him. Let's stop being selfish and mistreating what God has given us."

What a revelation! When this whole idea of owning and

belonging began to take shape, it was a powerful reality for Valerie. For one thing, it meant that her motivation should be to please God by pleasing her husband. God had given charge of John's body in sexual intimacy to Valerie. It was her responsibility to bring him happiness.

All this time, my thoughts have centered on all the ways that John has let me down, Valerie thought. *I've been so focused on blaming him for the ways he's neglected me and failed to meet my needs that I haven't thought about whether or not I was meeting his.*

Patricia closed her Bible and asked the ladies to stand for a closing prayer. "What you should clearly see from this study is God's lure for you," she said, taking a moment to look at each of the women in the room. "He wants you to read and understand His Word. Give Him something to work with. Your desire should be to make your mate happy knowing that God gave him to you. Begin to think of ways to make him feel good, to build up his self-esteem, to make him thank God for you. This means you have to get close to him. Learn his likes and his ideas about intimacy, and—" she paused and smiled mischievously– "make sure he receives a healthy dose of them."

The room started to buzz with giggling and talking as the women realized what she was saying God wanted them to do.

Patricia laughed and clasped her hands together, her delight obvious. "Now imagine your man reciprocating. The lure of the Lord is grace."

※　※　※

As Valerie drove home, she determined to read 1 Corinthians for herself. She sensed that God had a lot of work to do in her life. She felt God convicting her of sinful thoughts, a self-centered life, a holier-than-thou attitude, and a worldly view of intimacy in marriage. But, as conscious as she was now of her faults, she did not feel condemned. Instead, she felt confident that God's grace would help her change for the better.

As she studied 1 Corinthians over the next few weeks, she felt God reshaping her, showing her how to make her marriage God-honoring. Valerie realized instead of talking through her problems with her husband, she'd chosen to use her body as a weapon—a way to hurt her husband by saying "no." When Valerie had refused to be intimate with John, her actions spoke volumes. It was a way to say to John, "What have you done for me lately? I'm not here for you to be satisfied! My body is not yours! Show *me* a little affection. You are inadequate!"

Worst of all, Valerie realized, was that she'd felt completely justified in refusing her husband. She knew God had instructed John to love her like he would a weaker vessel. In fact, he was expected to be willing to give his very life for her. Those parts of the Scripture she knew.

But she'd never really taken her part—the Scriptures that commanded her to respect her husband—all that seriously. Valerie figured that keeping the true condition of their marriage secret from close friends was respect enough. When she felt convicted about not showing John respect, she'd counteract that feeling with the thought that he needed to do something to earn her respect. But that wasn't God's plan—and it wasn't sacrificial love.

Lord, I'm just beginning to see how badly we've gotten off-track, she prayed silently. *Thank You for pointing out these painful truths to me. I see now that I've been placing the blame for our failed marriage totally on John. I do believe that You've given the man special responsibility before You. John is to let Christ lead him, as he leads me. But that doesn't remove my responsibility for being who You'd have me to be. Please forgive me. Show us both how we can serve each other—and start with me. Help me to find ways to do something special for John. Help me to take care of my body and to be appealing to him. And most of all, Lord, let us recapture the spiritual and emotional closeness we used to share.*

She started to begin each day with a new prayer: "Lord,

you take over. My marriage is in your hands. I'm stepping out of your way now. I'm willing to obey. You're in charge. In Jesus' name, I truly pray. Amen."

Nine

Instructions for Success

Valerie waited anxiously on the couch, clasping and unclasping her hands nervously. She'd hurried home from work as soon as she could.

"Lord, I really need your help with this," she prayed softly. She didn't know how she was going to begin, but she was determined to talk to John about an upcoming marriage seminar at Faith Community Church based on the Fruit of the Spirit. She had decided that she would go alone if she had to. But, maybe, if they went together, they'd be able to work together to revive their marriage.

Valerie felt the tension in her neck muscles increasing as she heard the garage door opening. As John pulled his car into the driveway, she breathed a final, whispered prayer for help, then smoothed her hair and placed her hands in her lap.

Valerie took a deep breath as John walked in the door.

"Hi, John," she ventured.

Her husband jumped. It had been a long time since she'd met him when he came home from work.

"Sorry," she said, with a nervous laugh. A look of irritation flickered over his smooth, handsome face as he paused and turned to look at her.

"I—ah . . ." she fumbled for words, then decided to just say what was on her mind. "I know things between us haven't been that great for a while now—"

He raised his eyebrows at her as he put down his brief-case and crossed his arms.

"—Kind of an understatement, I guess. But I'd like to try to make things work. I'd like to try." She pushed a flyer about the retreat into his hand.

"You've heard about the marriage seminar at church that starts in a couple of weeks? I'm going to go."

He seemed unresponsive.

"Anyway, it would be great if you'd come too. I'm hoping it will help us."

John picked up his briefcase and turned toward his bed-room.

"It lasts for the next three weekends, but I'm hoping it'll be worth it," she said. "I—"

"I'll think about it," John mumbled as he walked away. Valerie watched his back as he left and prayed that he really would give it some thought.

❋   ❋   ❋

Valerie shifted nervously in her seat, wondering if John was going to come. The room was filling quickly with chat-tering couples filing into the fellowship hall auditorium for the marriage conference.

She checked her watch. They hadn't spoken much since she'd invited him to the conference. When they did, their conversations had been forced—about the weather, or house-hold repairs, or work. Still, it had been better than the bitter, electric silence between them over the last few months.

I hope he comes, she thought, looking around the room. *Lord, if he doesn't come, I'll be so embarrassed.* Everyone seemed so happy, their lives so perfect. But she knew that to everyone else, her life with John seemed that way.

Valerie chuckled dryly to herself. Her marriage was in such poor condition that she was attending a marriage conference by herself. Yet she was afraid of being embarrassed! She shook her head at the irony.

"Mind if I sit here?" Janice's voice interrupted her thoughts. "Tim had to work today, so I'm here alone." Valerie nodded and slid over, making room for her friend on the pew. "No problem," she said, knowing her friend had probably figured out why she was by herself. "Looks like I'm in the same situation."

Rev. Thomas stood to introduce Dr. Alex Matthews, a noted speaker, author, counselor, and authority on marriage. Valerie had heard him on the radio. This Fruit of the Spirit seminar was considered one of the best marriage seminars in the country.

Valerie's heart sank as Dr. Matthews took the podium. It looked like John wasn't coming.

Lord, this just seems to get more and more difficult, she thought. *But if I have to do this alone, give me strength.*

"Excuse me," John whispered, taking a seat next to her.

Valerie smiled slightly as she felt a wave of relief. His manner was businesslike, polite, almost impersonal as he nodded at her and placed his Bible and notebook on his lap. She felt no warmth between them. But he was here, and it was a start. Maybe he wanted to work things out, together. Maybe there was still hope for them. She closed her eyes and said a silent prayer of thanks.

Ushers passed out handouts that contained empty spaces for writing. "Our time together is going to be serious fun," Dr. Matthews said, opening his Bible and settling his notes on the podium. "In three sessions over the next three weeks, we'll be learning nine principles for a happier marriage. These are principles from Galatians 5:22–23," he said. "I'd like you to turn there with me."

When it seemed like most of the participants had found the passage, he asked everyone to stand and read it together.

"But the fruit of the Spirit is love, joy, peace, patience, kindness, goodness, faithfulness, gentleness and self-control."

As the audience settled into the plush seats, Dr. Matthews repeated each of the fruit names, pausing after each word for emphasis. "Love. Joy. Peace. Patience. Kindness. Goodness. Faithfulness. Gentleness. Self-Control."

"During our time together, we're going to discover that all of these fruits are available to us. In fact, it's God's will that we have all of them—He's not holding out on us!" he smiled. "Our problem is that we don't take the time to cultivate these gifts in our lives and marriages. But after today we will try and treat each other better. Right?" He nodded his head until the audience echoed him.

Valerie reached over and squeezed John's arm gently. She smiled nervously, hoping he'd sense her silent apology for her part in the condition of their marriage. He started slightly at her touch, but did not respond. "We are going to examine certain fruit together, because they hold hands with each other," Dr. Matthews continued. "Tonight, we're going to start with love, joy, and peace." His voice took on a playful tone. "Since I'm here with Christian folk, I know that the fruit I just named are easy pickings for you." He took off his glasses and wiggled his eyebrows. Everyone laughed. "So, some things you already are quite knowledgeable of. After this session, I hope you will practice them daily at home."

His style of delivery was conversational and witty. He had a mischievous smile that complimented his method of teaching. The pitch of his voice was comforting yet firm. When he spoke, he walked from one end of the podium to the other, stopping in the center to make a strong point. He was medium height, appeared to be in his mid-forties, and had salt-and-pepper hair with more pepper than salt.

John surveyed the crowded room, and then turned to face Valerie. "It looks as though everybody has turned out for this," he whispered "I wonder if anybody needs it as much as we do." Valerie nodded.

They turned their attention toward Dr. Matthews.

"I call this section 'What's Love Got to Do with It?'" He chuckled. "Oh yeah . . . I don't get out much, but I hear things. I always keep my eyes peeled for illustrations. In this case, I kept my ears peeled, as well."

He paused for a moment as the audience laughed. "What's love got to do with it? Everything! If any of you feel like you've lost your love for your mate, I don't want you to despair. God cares deeply for your marriage, and he wants to help you recapture that love you had. And he wants to place it on a firmer foundation than before."

Valerie couldn't help but look at John and wonder how they could turn the words they were hearing into a reality for their marriage. They'd been building their marriage on something. But whatever it was, it hadn't held up under the pressures they'd faced.

"Once Jesus is Lord of your life and your marriage, then you will possess the ability to love each other."

Valerie shook her head slowly. Was it really that simple?

Dr. Matthews leaned forward confidentially. "By the way, men, we are commanded to love our wives," he said in a stage whisper. "Women, you are commanded to respect your husbands."

He seemed to look directly at Valerie when he made that statement, she thought. But she convinced herself that she was merely feeling guilty about all the times she made it a point not to consider John, let alone respect him.

"I believe that God knows something about these two sexes he created," Dr. Matthews said. "God knows that women are more likely to love without being told to and less likely to respect." He flashed a hint of that mischievous grin. "Ladies, don't think you're off the hook, though. Look at your handout. In Titus 2:4, the apostle Paul tells the older women to teach the younger women to do what?" He cupped his hand to his ear and leaned forward as the women responded, "Love their husbands."

"Whoops—there it is!" he exclaimed. "So loving each other and respecting one another go hand in hand. But now that you know what you have to do, how do you translate that into truly loving your mate?"

Valerie's pen paused over her open notebook. This was what she needed—some practical teaching on how to make things work.

"First, you need to pray," Dr. Matthews said.

I know how to do this, Valerie thought, feeling a little disappointed to hear such simple advice.

"I don't just mean telling God what's wrong with your marriage, either," Dr. Matthews said, catching Valerie by surprise. "Pray for God's will for your marriage. Pray for your spiritual life, and for that of your spouse," he said. "Find out what's important to your wife or husband—that means you have to talk to one another— and pray for your spouse's concerns. His job, her job, his mother, her illness, whatever," he said, pausing behind the podium.

"I've found it is hard to have animosity, hatred, or disdain for someone you're bringing before God every day. You would have to be insincere with God to pull that off. And it's hard to hate someone you are praying with every day," he said. *"Pray."*

Valerie tried to remember the last time she and John had prayed together about anything. She realized that since they'd stopped eating meals together, they hadn't even said grace together in months. She remembered holding John's large, warm hand and hearing his deep, full voice telling their heavenly Father about their concerns. What would it take to cause them to pray together again?

"I've got a second instruction for you that relates to love," Dr. Matthews said, smiling broadly. "It's one that you'll remember from grade school." He leaned toward the audience. "Show and tell," he laughed. "Show and tell! It's one thing to know you are loved. It's quite another to *know* you are loved. Yes, this includes the sacrificial love, men. But it also includes the 'feel-good' variety—and that goes for men and women."

Valerie felt a little discouraged as she realized, yet again, how much work she and John really needed to do to recapture the closeness they'd felt before. There was a time when they used to show each other how much they cared. When they were committed to their marriage, expressing their love seemed easy. She remembered how she used to make a special effort to have John's favorite foods in the refrigerator. How she'd once had a CD by one of his favorite jazz artists delivered to him at work. The way he used to leave notes on her car, or how he liked to buy special gourmet coffee for her, even though he hated coffee. It wouldn't be too hard for her to start doing things like that again, she thought.

"Now, if someone is showing you love, you need to be open to receiving it. That's suggestion three," Dr. Matthews said. "When your spouse is telling you about his love, or when she's doing things to show you her love, you need to receive it at face value," he said. "Stay out of the giver's mind. Don't look for ulterior motives or trickery. God will reveal wrong intent or two-faced hearts."

Receive love, Valerie thought. *I remember how I used to thank John for doing kind things for me—just everyday things, like taking out the trash, or putting gas in my car, or leaving the porch light on for me when I was working late. But when we began fighting so much, I never took his kindness at face value. I always thought he had some sort of ulterior motive.*

"Now remember, these other things will come out of the first thing I told you," Dr. Matthews said. "Remember what I told you first? You have to do what?"

He cupped his ear and the audience responded in unison: "Pray!"

"How often?"

He cupped his ear as they shouted, "Every day!"

He smiled and said, "You're covered. What's love got to do with it? Everything. Now come on back in about twenty minutes, and we'll talk about joy."

Valerie and Janice slipped quickly out of the auditorium, hoping to avoid a long line in the ladies' room. As they walked along the corridor of the large church building, Valerie turned to Janice with a smile.

"He came!" she said, joy in her brown eyes. "I invited John to the conference a couple of weeks ago, but I didn't think he would come. I was pretty discouraged there for a few minutes."

Janice squeezed her friend's arm. "I know," she said, her voice full of sympathy. "I was praying that he'd come."

Valerie smiled. "Thank you. I've really appreciated the way you've supported me, Janice."

Janice nodded her head. "I'm your friend, Valerie. Anyway, what have you thought of the conference so far?"

"The more I hear, the more I realize how much responsibility I have for the state of my marriage. The funny thing, though, is that I don't feel condemned," Valerie searched for the right words. "Now that I can see the part I've played in some of the problems we're having, I feel . . . convicted. Challenged. Encouraged, maybe." She tried another word. "Empowered, almost."

Janice smiled. "That's a step in the right direction."

※   ※   ※

Valerie seated herself next to John just as Dr. Matthews began the next session.

Dr. Matthews stood in the center of the stage and waited for the audience to settle in.

"This marriage is not working," he moaned, his voice breaking with sorrow. "My marriage is not happy!" He stood silently looking out over the room, letting his words sink in.

"Have you ever said those words? Ever thought those words?" He asked the questions in a modulated tone as if he was having a one on one conversation with each person in the room. He resumed his stride back and forth across the stage. "There are a lot of reasons for unhappiness in marriage. I'd like to talk to you about an especially important one." He paused. "See, a lot of times we want to say it's all about the other person," he said. "It's your husband's fault you can't be happy in your marriage. Or if your wife would just do right, you'd be happy in your marriage. If she'd just tell her mother to stop coming over unannounced, things would be OK," he smiled. "If he would just make sure he shared in the household chores, you might be happy together." He laughed. "Now, for some of you, there's some truth to that! But for others, unrealistic and unbiblical expectations are preventing you from having joy."

Dr. Matthews repeated himself. "Our unrealistic and unbiblical expectations are often the reason for our unhappiness in our marriages."

"Now, just in case you wonder what I mean by an 'unrealistic and unbiblical expectations,' I'm going to give you a few examples," he said. "Ushers, stand by the doors, please. I'm going to step on some toes here, and I don't want anyone leaving before I'm finished." The audience chuckled.

"OK, here goes. It is unrealistic and unbiblical to expect your spouse to look like Denzel or Halle for as long as you both shall live," he said, stopping as a wave of laughter passed through the crowd.

"It is unrealistic and unbiblical to expect your spouse to read your mind, to understand what you are thinking without your ever needing to communicate with one another," Dr. Matthews continued, a serious expression replacing the grin on his face. "It is unrealistic and unbiblical to expect that everything will always go your way, and that you'll have a happy marriage without having to work out your conflicts, without having to submit to one another," he said.

Valerie squirmed in her seat and snuck a furtive glance at her husband. John was taking notes. His friend, Melvin Fletcher, who had gotten a seat next to him, said something humorous. He smiled and kept writing.

How often have I had unrealistic expectations of my husband? Valerie wondered. *How often have I chosen to focus on how I thought things should be, instead of thinking of ways I could be content with what we had? Instead of thinking about how I could make things better. It's no wonder I've been so unhappy.*

"The first step to happiness in your marriage is joy in your heart," Dr. Matthews said. "And, guess what? As Christians . . ."

It was obvious Dr. Matthews enjoyed the dramatic. He stood in the center of the stage and pointed to each area of the room as he said, "you . . . you . . . and *you* already possess that joy."

"You see, when we stop experiencing our God-given joy —joy that is not dependent on our circumstances—we start to have unreasonable expectations for our mates. We have a choice, but a lot of times we choose to look to our mate instead of to God for our deepest joy. And that's when we begin to whine about not having a happy marriage. Now, I'd like you to write this down. There are two things we need to address. Number one, we blame our unhappiness on our situation—on the marriage. But the truth is, we are looking for fulfillment from our mates in areas that we should draw on the joy from within to satisfy. We have unmet emotional and spiritual needs in some areas, and we want our mates to fill the void. Ladies and gentlemen, what you are doing is unjust to your mate, and will damage your marriage. If I'm talking to you this evening, I encourage you to think about this before it's too late."

Valerie realized that she'd allowed the areas where she and John disagreed to overshadow all of the commonalities they shared. In time, she couldn't even remember why she'd ever thought they were compatible enough to marry. She sighed and added Dr. Matthews' first point to her notes.

"Point two," Dr. Matthews continued. "Until you claim your inner joy which comes from the Lord, and which you have in situations that are bad and situations that are sad—until you claim that joy, there is not a man or woman on this earth who can ever satisfy you."

Valerie and John stood as the audience rose, applauding.

"Joy makes the difference!" Dr. Matthews said. "I believe denying it, squelching it, ignoring it is an affront to God who gave it. God supplied it for every circumstance, and He has given it to us in abundance—in surplus. Now, let's look at what joy is." He directed the audience to turn to Romans 12:12, where Paul instructs the Romans to "be joyful in hope, patient in affliction, faithful in prayer."

"Have you done these things in your marriage?" Dr. Matthews asked. "Have you been joyful in hope?"

He suggested his listeners take a moment to read verses 9–17. During this interlude, Valerie leaned toward John.

"He really has an amazing style of delivery, doesn't he?" Valerie whispered, hoping to start a conversation. "I mean, we've been here for two hours on a Saturday afternoon, but everyone seems to be holding on to his every word. I don't think anybody's left since he began."

John looked up from his notes. "He definitely knows how to handle an audience. But I think his words are making the real impact."

Then John did something unexpected. He turned to his wife and touched her arm lightly.

"Listening to him, I see areas in our marriage where I could have acted differently, treated you differently." John was looking directly into Valerie's eyes—something he hadn't done for months.

Valerie's lips parted in surprise. Taken aback, she didn't know how to respond. Should she tell John about some of her own failings in their marriage? Should she tell him she accepted his apology? Uncertain, she nodded and patted his hand on her arm.

They turned their attention back to the stage, where Dr. Matthews was making his final comments about joy. "The surplus of joy God promises is there even during the painful periods during your marriage. In fact, your joy should exhibit itself in several ways."

There was a list in their handout. Valerie noticed John had already looked at his and made notes on it. Dr. Matthews began going down the list. "A believer's joy should be great, abundant, and exceeding." He smiled. "Yes, those are three ways of saying the same thing. God honors marriage, and He wants it to be a source of joy. But even when it isn't, He is your ultimate source of joy. This means that the couples here should be rejoicing, during good times and bad."

"If you take your joy home with you, you might find that elusive happiness you've been looking for," he said, dismissing the audience for a brief break.

Valerie sat thinking about her conversation with John as he and Melvin left to stretch their legs between sessions. She was still a bit stunned; ruffled even. They had touched for the first time in months—and he'd spoken kind words to her. He'd confessed that he hadn't always done his best in their marriage—even though he surely knew at least something about her involvement with Curtis. Did this mean there was still some hope that they could work out the problems in their marriage together? Maybe this was a start.

Valerie breathed a quick prayer of thanks as her husband rejoined her in the sanctuary.

❈   ❈   ❈

"Now, I'm just going to hold you for a few more minutes. This is a short session, but I don't want you to think it's not important," Dr. Matthews said. "I want to talk a little about peace. Have you ever gone through a rough time and had someone ask you how you could be so calm in the midst of your crisis?"

He stood at one side of the podium, leaning against it. "Peace is available to every Christian who seeks it from

God—and like love, like joy, it can be yours regardless of the circumstances you find yourself in. No matter the test, no matter the trial—whether these are the best of times or the worst of times—it doesn't change the reality of your peace."

"Like all of the fruit, we have to choose to reject peace. So my question to you is, 'Does peace reign in your home?' Are you doing everything you can to live peacefully with your spouse, like Romans 12:18 says?"

Valerie shifted guiltily in her seat. She knew she was guilty of not using the other two fruit they'd studied that day, but she felt like she'd really neglected peace. The only time she and John had been at peace lately was when they didn't talk to each other. That was not a true peace—that was a truce in the middle of a Cold War. She glanced at John. What were they going to do?

As he had done when he talked about the other fruit, Dr. Matthews told the audience that peace was theirs to have, if they but pursued it. He walked to the edge of the stage. "Now, I'm going to give you three ways to pursue peace, and then I'm going to let you go," he said. "So write these down."

"First," he said, "remember that you have to connect to the source. Stop trying to force peace into your marriage. Plug into your source. Tell the Lord you're willing to work for peace in your life, and peace in your home, and mean it. Ask him to show you ways to be a source of peace. Then, plug into your spouse."

"Second," Dr. Matthews said, "remember that you and your spouse are on the same team! You are working together to make your marriage better. God gave you to each other, so you have to talk to one another to make things work. You have to be willing to change, to accommodate one another, to put the other's needs before your own."

Valerie paused. When had she tried to change her habits and attitudes to accommodate John? When had she sacrificed her desires for his?

"Finally, stop trying to be right all the time," he said. "My wife will tell you that this one's a tough one for me! I just love—" he drew out the word dramatically—"to be right." The audience laughed appreciatively.

"So I decided to memorize a little poem, for the sake of peace in my home. This poem is by the 20th-century poet and playwright Ogden Nash. And whenever I get out of line, Ceci asks me to recite it."

He stood in the middle of the platform, arms straight at his sides like a child speaking his "piece" at the annual Easter program.

"If you want your marriage to sizzle
With love in the loving cup,
Whenever you're wrong admit it;
Whenever you're right, shut up!"

He emphasized the last two words with a shout. The audience roared with laughter.

"All right, that will give you plenty of 'homework' before we get together next week. Love, joy, and peace. Take some time to think about how they can be a part of your marriage. Talk to your spouse about how they can be part of your marriage. And talk to God constantly about it. All right, let's pray and go on home. I'll see you next week."

Ten

A LOOK BACK

Over the next week, Valerie tried to think of ways that she could apply the things she'd heard at the conference to her marriage. Even though they still weren't talking much, she prayed for John every day. Valerie asked the Lord to bless her husband at work, to keep John safe as he traveled to his different sales regions, to grant him favor with his clients. She asked God to bless their marriage and give them strength to work through their problems. She thanked God for moving on each of their hearts during the conference. She thought about joy, and repented of expecting her husband to provide for her emotional health in ways that only God could.

After struggling to think of some ways to show John that she loved him, Valerie decided to buy a few of her husband's favorite foods. Although they never ate together, she hoped that if John saw some of his favorite treats in the refrigerator and pantry, he'd recognize her gesture of peace. And she tried not to let the little things—like the way he tossed the towels in a heap on the laundry room floor or the fact that he always left his shoes by the couch—get to her. Instead, she tried to be thankful that as bad as things were, she and her husband were both interested in working on their marriage.

And Valerie decided that even though John didn't really acknowledge her efforts, and even though he actually seemed unusually busy and distant, his coming to the marriage conference had been a start.

Besides, she told herself as she folded the laundry one evening, *it took a long time for things to become as bad as they are. I can't expect one weekend seminar to change things overnight.*

Still, she couldn't shake a slight unease she felt. John had seemed very sincere when he apologized to her at the conference. Why hadn't they spoken about it since then? Why did he seem so preoccupied? When they were discussing household matters, it seemed like his body was present, but his mind was elsewhere. She realized that he'd been coming home later and later several evenings, and . . . recalled hearing his deep, rumbling laugh from the guest bedroom as he talked on the phone late at night.

Valerie shook her head as she shook one of John's shirts. Was she actually thinking that John might be having an affair? She chuckled ruefully and tried to silence the thought. He wouldn't risk being caught, would he? He'd been so angry when he'd suspected her relationship with Curtis, there was really no reason for him to do anything like that.

Unless he was trying to get his revenge on her.

Unless he was planning to leave her, and he was going to the conference so he could say he'd tried to make things work, one last time.

Unless his apology at the conference was his way of telling her it was over, and he felt badly about it.

With tears in her eyes, Valerie knelt beside a stack of John's shirts and tried to pray.

※　※　※

"Well, it looks like I didn't beat up on you too badly last week," Dr. Matthews laughed as he opened the second weekend of Fruit of the Spirit seminars. His eyes wandered over the audience assembled in the fellowship hall auditorium. "Most of you came back for more! I hope that's because you've exhausted the possibilities of love, joy, and peace, and things have been so loving and happy and full of peace, you just don't know what to do with yourselves." The audience caught his gentle humor and chuckled softly. "And so even though your marriages are now pretty much close to perfect, you just had to come and find out if there was anything else you needed to know."

"Well, today is your day. We're going to get started now on kindness, goodness, and gentleness." He directed everyone to pull out their notes.

"Let's start with kindness and goodness," Dr. Matthews said, leaning on the podium. "When was the last time you said something kind to your mate? When was the last time you asked yourself, 'Am I a good husband?' 'Am I a good wife?'"

Valerie sensed Dr. Matthews looking in her direction and nodded in response to the question. She couldn't recall the last time she'd said anything kind to John. And the Bible study at Patricia's had taught her that she was usually only "good" to John when it benefited her somehow.

"You know," Dr. Matthews said, clapping his hands together to emphasize his thought, "we are kind to someone we love. We are good, good from deep inside, when we are trying to please God by loving our spouses. Being kind takes effort. Being good takes sacrifice—but your marriage is worth it."

Valerie had been fighting her discouragement over the last couple of days. She almost hadn't bothered to come to the second conference session. If both she and her husband had cheated, was her marriage worth much effort?

"Kindness can also lead to forgiveness," Dr. Matthews continued. "Got any forgiving you need to do? Well, start being kind to the person you need to forgive. With God's help, be good to that person, and it will help that forgiveness along."

Valerie snuck a look at John, who had come to the conference from work—or that's what she thought he'd said.
Had he forgiven her for what he had learned about her meetings with Curtis, or was he paying her back? Was he having
an affair?

"I don't know what kinds of things have hurt the marriages here," Dr. Matthews said, "but I know there are people
here who need to forgive each other. And like I said, one
way to start doing that is by being kind. I'd like each of you
to turn to your mate and say something kind."

Valerie sensed that John was as uncomfortable as she was
as they turned to face each other. *How had something that had
once felt so natural become a source of discomfort?*

She smiled, wondering if her husband was having the
same thought.

He sighed. "Valerie, I—" he paused as his eyes searched
her face. "I think you have . . . beautiful lips." She blushed,
surprising them both. It had been a long time since a compliment had passed between them.

"John," Valerie said, "I love your eyes." She fluttered her
lashes flirtatiously at him, and they laughed together. She felt
a little of the chemistry they'd shared during happier times.

Dr. Matthews was closing the segment on kindness and
goodness, but Valerie's mind was just warming up. Dr.
Matthews' exercise caused her to remember other things she
liked about her husband. She absolutely loved John's sense
of humor, his spontaneity, his smile, and his hands. Valerie
remembered her fascination with Curtis' hands. Was she
really longing for John but crediting Curtis with his attri-
butes? And if John had found someone else, did it really
matter anymore? She struggled again between her hopes for
her marriage and her suspicion that it might already be over.

Valerie knew kindness consisted of more than just compliments on lips and eyes. But again, it was a start. And
maybe she could think of some other ways to be kind and
good to her husband.

❊ ❊ ❊

When Dr. Matthews dismissed the audience for a short break, Valerie was relieved. As interesting as the sessions were, their intensity drained her a bit.

She ran into Janice at the refreshments table at the back of the fellowship hall.

"Hey, Janice," Valerie said, noticing that Janice's husband, Tim, was with her today. "Hey, Tim, it's nice to see you."

Tim grinned. "Well, my wife—" he shot a playful glance at Janice "—just couldn't stop talking about 'Dr. Matthews said this, Dr. Matthews said that,' so I thought I'd better come and hear some of it for myself." He grabbed two donuts before heading back to his seat.

Janice shook her head and smiled. "Tim took off work to come hear the sessions today."

Valerie laughed at her friend's joy. "You guys sure seem to be doing well."

"Speaking of doing well," Janice said, raising an eyebrow, "I thought I saw you and your husband flirting a little bit this morning." She fanned herself dramatically. "Girl, do you need to share a praise report with somebody?"

Valerie rolled her eyes, but she couldn't hide the wide smile spreading across her face. "Girl, please!" she leaned forward confidentially. "Nothing yet. Believe me, I'm just as surprised as you are. Although, I have to say, talking to John that way felt good. It really did. But I just keep fighting to keep my balance. First I'm hopeful, then something happens to discourage me." She felt tears welling in her eyes and blinked them away. "So don't stop praying yet." She wondered if she should confide her fears about John having an affair, then stopped herself. After all, they were mere suspicions. And maybe they were just grounded in her fears about her own weaknesses.

Janice patted her friend's arm and nodded sympathetically. "Do you want to talk about this over dinner tonight? We could go to Ciao Bella. We haven't been there for a while."

"Well, if things go well today, I think I'm going to ask John if he'd like to go out to dinner tonight, just to talk," Valerie said. "I think I'll take a rain check for now."

"I'd better find my seat again," Janice said, "but I'll be praying that you and John have a great dinner this evening." She hugged her friend.

✳ ✳ ✳

"Dolcezza," Dr. Matthews said in a deep voice, raising his eyebrows suggestively at no one in particular. "Docilidad," he said, smiling as the audience chuckled at his performance. "Douceur," he continued, voice deepening. "Prautes. Anvath."

He paused and extended his arms toward the audience. "Gentleness," he said. "Gentleness."

Dr. Matthews let the audience absorb the moment before he started pacing. "You see, gentleness is a beautiful word. It has a calming effect, no matter what language you say it in—Italian, Spanish, French, Greek, Hebrew. Now we're going to do a little exercise here. I want you to turn to your spouse and say the word 'gentleness,'" he said.

John and Valerie faced one another. "Gentleness," John said.

Valerie smiled. "Gentleness," she whispered.

Dr. Matthews' voice broke into their interchange. "Now, I want you to say the same word, but this time I want you to scream it angrily."

They faced each other again, and John shook his head. "OK, enough audience participation already," he said. They laughed as they heard the screaming couples around them, and Valerie felt another small twinge of hope.

Dr. Matthews laughed. "It's hard to do, isn't it? Just as the word 'gentleness' is hard to say in an angry tone, so is it diffi-

cult to be gentle and angry at the same time." He smiled and
stroked his chin.

"Wonder if God somehow knew that?"

John leaned over and whispered, "He really knows how
to put people at ease and teach them at the same time." Valerie nodded. As John returned his gaze to his notes, Valerie
looked at her husband and felt an unexpected warmth
toward him. She patted his knee lightly.

"Have you ever cared tenderly for something?" Dr.
Matthews gave the question a moment to sink in. "How
many gardeners do we have here tonight?" Some in the
group raised their hands. "How many pet lovers?" Several
hands went up. "Consider the tender care you give your
garden, and especially your pet. That's what gentleness is—
it's tender care. And although you'd never go without water-
ing your garden or brushing your pet, sometimes we forget
that our spouses need that kind of tender care every day."

Tender care, Valerie thought. *I can remember when that felt like
second nature to John and me.*

She remembered rushing home from work to prepare
dinner—and to prepare herself. But over the years, as she
and John settled into their marriage, her moments of affection appeared less frequently—and sometimes came with
strings attached when they did. Finally, Valerie realized,
she'd stopped making any special effort at all.

She'd forgotten that John had looked forward to coming
home to her. Sometimes he'd call her at her office and tell
her not to cook dinner because he was bringing dinner
home, or he was taking her out. John told her he loved her
and his actions showed it too.

Valerie shook her head. When had they allowed mean-
spiritedness to replace the spirit of gentleness in their home?
And how had things gotten so bad that she'd turned to another man—a stranger she met in the park and really didn't
know—as an escape?

Dr. Matthews' voice broke into her thoughts. "Most of

the biblical references to gentleness are related to the way God interacts with us," he said. "But since it is one of the Spirit's fruit, Christians are expected to follow God's example and extend it to others. And that's your 'homework' this week," he said before praying and dismissing them. "Be kind, good, and gentle to one another. I'll see you next Saturday."

Valerie rose quickly after the prayer, hoping to catch John before he headed to his car.

"John," she said, touching his arm lightly, "I wondered if you might want to have dinner tonight."

John paused, a look of discomfort flashing across his face. His eyes darted around the room as if he hoped an excuse would magically appear there.

Confused, she tried again. "I thought maybe we could talk about the session—"

"I can't," he said, interrupting her. "I'm sorry, Valerie, I . . . Melvin and I were planning to shoot some hoops at the gym tonight." He scooped up his Bible and notes and headed for the door.

His response caught her off guard. He'd seemed so attentive during the sessions, and she'd really hoped that they would give them a chance to talk about how they could rebuild their marriage. The hope she'd felt dissolved in doubt again.

As she walked across the parking lot to her car, Valerie wondered how easy it would be for John to meet a woman instead of meeting Melvin. Melvin could be a convenient excuse to cover his real plans. After all, he hadn't responded at all to some of the changes she'd made since the first seminar. He still seemed uneasy around her. Maybe attending the seminar was just some sort of façade, some charade to make himself look good at church, or to throw her off his trail. Maybe she'd been fooling herself. Maybe she hadn't been the only one who'd wanted out of their marriage. Maybe she should just give up and let go.

Valerie squelched the thought. Weren't their marriage vows—or at least the false front she and her husband had created—too important to John to risk being seen with someone else? She felt her guilty feelings settling over her again. It hadn't been that way for her and Curtis.

As she pulled into her driveway and faced another evening alone with the television and her own thoughts, Valerie wondered if it was too late to call Janice and go to dinner. Then she realized that she was tired and weak and didn't feel like talking, not even to her best friend.

※　※　※

The phone rang just as Valerie had settled herself in her bed with a magazine. She sighed and considered not answering. Then, hoping it might be Janice, she decided to pick it up.

"Hello?" she said, cradling the phone between her ear and shoulder.

"Valerie, it's good to hear your voice."

It was Curtis.

Valerie knew that she should probably hang up the phone, but the sound of his smooth, mellow voice brought back all of the desire she'd tried to quench, the memories she still fought to reject. She was grateful that he was only on the phone and not in the same room. In her sadness and longing, part of her wanted to start where they'd left off. For a moment, the idea of repairing her marriage seemed less appealing than the idea of escaping it.

"How are you?" she asked, lowering her voice.

"I'm doing well. I would be doing better, if I could see you. I've thought about you a lot over the last few months."

She felt a rush of warmth. He'd thought of her.

"You've . . . ah . . . you've been on my mind too," she said, fighting for her composure. "How's the new job going?"

"Going well. Can't complain. In fact, things in my life

would be exactly as I'd wanted them, if a certain lady had considered taking me up on my offer to relocate with me. But maybe it's not too late . . ." His voice trailed off, leaving her fumbling for an answer to his question.

"Curtis, my doing that would have been much too complicated for everyone."

"Valerie." He drew out the syllables of her name. "How complicated would it be just to pack a suitcase and be ready when I come by for you?" he laughed softly. "We wouldn't have to live together," he said, his tone playful. "And even if we did, well, we're adults. We'd be able to contain ourselves until God freed you from your marriage. I can resist you, you know," he said jokingly.

Valerie remembered that painful day in the park when all she'd wanted was to feel Curtis' lips on hers, wanted to stand there in his embrace forever. Yet he'd walked away. "How well I know," she said ruefully.

"I've been praying for you, asking God to release you from your marriage and let us be together."

His mention of God and prayer jarred her. "Curtis, I'm still married. And I vowed before God that I would do whatever I could to make my life with John, my marriage with John, work out. That's what I'm supposed to be praying for."

Curtis' voice took on a patient, soothing tone. "Valerie, Valerie. We've talked about this," he said. "Sometimes God lets you out of a bad mistake. He freed me, and He's still blessing me every day. I believe He wants us together, or I would never have run into you at Sycamore Park. You can't tell me that was random, that we were both just supposed to keep walking."

A stream of silent tears slipped down Valerie's face. She felt her resolve crumbling.

"Valerie, when can I see you? How about this weekend? We can meet at the place where we first discovered each other."

"Oh, Curtis . . . I'm not sure that would be such a good

idea. We ended this once, maybe we should let it go, while
. . ." Valerie hesitated, realizing that she was at a point of decision. *While I can still say no,* she thought. Something in her
wanted to see Curtis, wondered if they could really have a
good relationship. Even over the phone, he made her feel so
alive. It was like he was caressing her with his very words.

How can this be? she wondered, realizing that she knew so
little about him, realizing that there was only the promise of
something between them. What she had with John was
deeper, flawed though it was. Had she tried hard enough to
make their marriage work? Would she be able to leave her
guilt if she stopped trying to fix what was so badly broken?
Couldn't she just get a fresh start?

"I can't give you an answer now, Curtis," Valerie said,
tears in her voice. "I need to think and pray."

"I understand, and that's what I want you to do," Curtis
said soothingly. "Look deep inside, Valerie. I'll call you later
to find out what you decide. While you're thinking, think of
this—I don't want to walk away by myself again. At least, I
want to know where we're headed."

Eleven

A Confrontation

Janice commented on the large number of cars in the parking lot as she and Valerie pulled up to Ciao Bella after Wednesday night Bible study.

"It looks like everyone had the same idea we did," she said, letting Valerie out at the door before pulling away to park the car. "I'm glad we made a reservation."

Valerie nodded and went into the foyer. The restaurant was almost always crowded. Its Italian décor and ambience were as responsible for its popularity as its delicious food. Waiters greeted diners in an entry foyer where the walls were painted with murals recalling bright scenes of a 19th-century-era canal in Venice, complete with riders and gondoliers. Italian music floated soothingly through hidden speakers that gave the impression the sound came from the wall paintings, lending life and authenticity to the already vibrant scenes.

The eating area consisted of rooms with a romantic ambience that only seated four. Cozy alcoves along one wall provided intimate spaces. The main floor housed tables for informal gatherings, and there were banquet rooms available for large parties.

As soon as they'd been seated, Valerie sensed a change in Janice's manner. She seemed uninterested in the idle chatter they'd made about the Bible study during the ride to the restaurant and in the entryway as they'd waited. "Valerie," she said, folding her hands on the table, "how are you and John doing?"

"Oh, about the same," Valerie said, choosing not to mention the small signs of progress she'd seen during the conference. She sighed and settled into the cushion of her camelback chair. "The conference has been a real eye-opener for me, though," she said, sipping her lemonade.

"Me too," Janice agreed. "Tim and I have been trying to talk through some of the things we've been learning." She stirred her coffee, then looked up. "So, did you guys end up going out after the seminar Saturday?"

Valerie sighed. "No. I asked him to, but he said that he and Melvin had made plans to go to the gym after the seminar."

"That's funny," Janice said. "I saw Melvin in the parking lot after the seminar when I went back to the church to get some visitor cards I had to log for the hospitality committee. I drove all the way home before I realized I'd forgotten them." Janice paused, panic flashing over her face as she realized her blunder. "But maybe their plans changed and John went alone."

Valerie laughed sarcastically. "Maybe we're doing worse than I thought."

Janice shook her head. "I'm sure it's nothing. What about Curtis? Heard any more from him?"

Valerie started at her friend's question. How could Janice know that Curtis was back? Then she realized Janice didn't know, but her reaction gave it away. Janice suddenly excused herself.

"I'll be right back," she said.

When she returned, Dr. Matthews was with her. Valerie was surprised, but pleasantly so. Janice explained that she had asked him to join them.

"Dr. Matthews flew in early this week, because he's doing a couple of book signings in the area," she said. "I thought sharing a meal might give us a chance to pick his brain," she joked as they took their seats.

Janice gestured toward Valerie as she made the introduction. "Dr. Matthews, this is my friend Valerie Mitchell."

"Hello, Valerie." Dr. Matthews shook her hand and smiled. "I've seen you at the conference."

"Yes," Janice replied for her. "We were just discussing the conference."

"Well," he said, skimming the menu and making a quick selection, "what have you thought about the conference so far?" He chuckled, knowing he'd caught them off guard. "Be honest with me. I'm not fishing for compliments. I would really like to know what you think. I would like to know if the teaching has made an impact on you." He looked directly at Valerie. "Has it helped you?"

Valerie smiled. "Yes, it has helped me very much. I was just going to tell Janice that I plan to incorporate what you have said into my own marriage."

"That's what I pray everyone will do. I was happy to see both you and your husband attending the sessions."

After the waiter refilled their beverages and took their orders, Janice dropped a bomb.

She turned to Valerie as if they were still alone. "Now tell me, Valerie," she said firmly, "have you heard any more from Curtis?"

Valerie felt a wave of angry heat pass over her.

"Janice!" she gasped in disbelief. "Let's not bore Dr. Matthews with that. I am sure he would rather talk about something else."

Valerie felt ambushed, betrayed. What was Janice thinking? There they sat with a world-renowned speaker and Janice wanted to discuss her relationship with Curtis. Valerie rifled through her purse, hunting for her car keys. Then she realized they'd come to the restaurant in Janice's car. Had

Janice been planning this all week? Valerie fumbled for her
cell phone. Maybe she could call a cab.

Valerie looked up, searching for the nearest exit. Then
she noticed the tears welling in Janice's eyes.

"Valerie, I'm sorry," she said, reaching for her friend's
hand. "I don't want to embarrass you. I don't want you to feel
trapped. But I am concerned about you. I am worried about
your marriage. I'm your friend, Valerie, and I just don't want
to see you make a mistake you can't undo."

Dr. Matthews looked searchingly at Valerie. "Look, I
don't want you to be ashamed," he said. "Janice just asked me
to talk to you because she thought maybe I could help."

He took another sip of his coffee, and then continued.
"If you'd like, we can talk about this. If not, we can drop it."

Valerie shrugged her shoulders and bit her lip, hoping
the tears in her eyes wouldn't roll down her cheeks. She lowered her eyes to her hands, clasped in her lap.

"I could tell that you and your husband were not happy
when I noticed you the second day of the conference," Dr.
Matthews said.

"That obvious, huh?" Valerie whispered, ashamed.

"Oh, don't be concerned, Valerie. I have a gift for that,
and I pray for it. Both you and your husband looked fine, but
I always ask God to show me a couple who needs His miraculous help in their lives to save their marriage. This time, He
showed me you."

Just then their food arrived. Dr. Matthews paused and
blessed it, and they began eating.

"I want to tell you something that I think will be helpful
to you," he said, twirling his fork in his pasta. "Before there
were the conferences, the lectures, and the books, I was a
man whose marriage was in deep trouble."

Valerie looked at him quizzically. Dr. Matthews in a
troubled marriage?

"Oh, yes," he said, answering her unasked question. "I
had decided that I didn't need to be married, didn't need my

wife. Even though neither of us had the guts to leave the marriage, I couldn't stand her, and she couldn't stand me."

He chuckled at the memory. "I'm laughing now, but at the time it was far from funny. I think that it was really just a matter of time before one of us had an affair. I was dangerously close, but God turned me around.

"Now, I was a Christian then. As a matter of fact, I was in seminary at the time. One day, an encounter with this 'other woman' made me realize how very close I was to jeopardizing my marriage, my future ministry, the life my wife and I had worked so hard to build together."

Valerie was surprised. His situation was very similar to hers.

"I was exhausted, and I didn't know what to do. I was, frankly, desperate," Dr. Matthews continued. "I was so tired of feeling guilty, of fighting between pleasing God and indulging my flesh," he shook his head at the memory. "I found myself on my knees in the campus chapel one evening, crying out to God, begging Him to save my marriage, to show me what I was doing wrong and save me from the problems I was causing myself."

"So what did you do? You prayed, and then what did you do?" Valerie leaned forward, anticipating his answer to her question.

Dr. Matthews nodded, smiling at her eagerness to hear his answer. "Well, it was a process. There weren't any quick fixes, and it took some real time and some serious effort to make our marriage work. It's all been worth it, though," he said. "And God has used our 'baggage' to help other people," he smiled.

"Some of the answers were straightforward, even though they weren't all easy." He stopped for a mouthful of pasta, then dabbed at his lips with his napkin.

"The first thing I did was to cut off all contact with this woman I was becoming attached to," he said. "I realized that if I was really serious about my marriage, I had to focus my attention, my energy, my affection, my daydreaming—" he sipped his coffee, "—back on Ceci, my wife. It wasn't easy, but it was liberating," he said. "I ended the conflict I was having with myself and focused on my choice to work on my relationship with Ceci."

Dr. Matthews leaned back in his chair. "Now, you ladies know I'm only sharing all my 'stuff' because I'm hoping it will help you," he said, laughing softly. "And only because I have Ceci's permission to go around talking about our business."

Janice smiled. "We really appreciate it too," she said. "It helps to know that everybody struggles sometimes."

"The next thing I did was to come clean with my wife, and to tell her that I wanted to work things out," he said. "I was afraid that she'd leave me, but I didn't want to try to re-build our marriage on the foundation of anything other than the truth."

Valerie wondered how John would respond if he knew the whole truth about her and Curtis. She wondered if there would end up being more "truth" to tell him. She wondered if she had the strength to even try.

"The next thing we did was even more humbling, if you can imagine," he said. "My wife and I went to a Christian marriage counselor." He smiled at the memory. "Now I'm a Christian marriage counselor, but at the time, I couldn't imagine going to a stranger to ask for help with my marriage. After all," he said, taking on a snooty, affected tone, "I was a Christian, a seminary student, even! Surely a budding theo-logian, a seminarian, an up-and-coming young minister should be able to handle something as simple as marriage on his own!"

Valerie and Janice shared a knowing look.

"Well, that's an illusion," Dr. Matthews said. "And illusion is a nice word for 'lie.' The fact is, my wife and I had married thinking that somehow romantic love would be enough to sustain a lifelong relationship." He paused. "It's a nice thought, but it's just not true. And a lot of couples, even

Christian couples, don't want to develop the coping skills, don't want to adapt themselves, don't want to make the adjustments or do the personal growth that helps them have a healthy marriage, even when things aren't all champagne and chocolate-covered strawberries," he said. "Ceci and I realized that our way of doing things wasn't working, and that if we wanted to learn a better way, we needed some outside help."

Valerie wondered if John would be interested in counseling. She couldn't see herself unburdening their troubles to a stranger. But if someone like Dr. Matthews had once needed a counselor . . .

Before Dr. Matthews could continue, the waiter arrived with a dessert tray. They ordered in a hurry so he could continue his story.

"Finally, and probably most importantly, I kept praying and asking for guidance, and I did what I am teaching you now. I was in a course on Galatians at the time, and I decided to apply the fruit of God's Holy Spirit to my marriage. It was not some great master plan I had. I just really wanted my wife to know that I had changed. See, God changed my heart and my thinking as soon as I asked Him. He knew I really loved my wife, and He created a desire in me for that one woman that can only be described as miraculous, considering that at one time I'd wanted to leave her," he said.

"By the way, that really was a miracle. As a counselor, I know now that the journey back to feeling affectionate toward one another is a long one for many couples." He reached for a dessert fork and took a bite of his tiramisu. "Anyway, we were a couple of poor grad students, so I couldn't purchase a big, fancy gift for her. In retrospect, I realize that the one I did come up with was better—and like I said, it wasn't my idea. I decided that I'd choose a different fruit of the Spirit each month, and I'd try to apply it to my interactions with my wife.

"So, you see, I'm not trying to teach anyone anything

that I haven't had to learn myself," he said. "I can teach about the fruit of the Spirit not because of my doctorate in theology, not because of my doctorate in counseling, but because of God's answer to a simple prayer. I experienced Him in ways far beyond what I had asked and certainly more than my confused mind could ever have thought. God doesn't half do anything," Dr. Matthews said, finishing his dessert. "He uses the simplest of concepts to solve some of our most complex problems." He glanced at his watch. "I need to leave soon, but I'd like to leave you ladies with one more thing," he said, pulling a pamphlet out of the breast pocket of his suit and sliding it across the table toward Valerie.

"Ceci and I conduct an annual marriage cruise," he said. "It is a very intimate bonding experience. Couples have truly been helped and recognize they have been freed to sincerely love each other when they leave the conference. We get a lot of letters from couples who have been helped, but we also conduct our own annual follow-up for two years. And I have seen amazing results, to the glory of God. Valerie, you and your husband should consider joining us on our next cruise."

"I would love to," she said, intrigued, "but we'll have to see. My marriage is not in the best shape right now."

"Don't give up," he said, motioning for his check. "God will honor all the effort you put into your marriage. I've seen it in my own life and in the lives of hundreds of others."

❋   ❋   ❋

Janice apologized to Valerie yet another time as she drove her back to the church parking lot to pick up her car.

"Valerie, I'm sorry that I had to confront you this way, but I'm your friend and I love you," she said. "I hope you can see that."

Valerie nodded from the passenger seat. "I know you care about me, Janice," she said. "Wasn't that a great story Dr. Matthews shared?"

Janice smiled, but clearly wasn't ready to drop the subject she'd brought up earlier that evening. "Valerie," she asked again in a very firm tone, "what about Curtis?"

Valerie sensed Janice's concern for her yet again. She clearly wasn't asking just to be in on the latest gossip. She could tell her friend wasn't about to giggle with her over this attractive man who was so interested in her. She didn't really want to subject herself to Janice's disapproval, but another part of her really wanted to unburden herself.

Valerie sighed. "Curtis did call. He told me he'll be going back to Seattle next weekend, and wanted to know if I had changed my mind about going with him."

"What did you tell him?" Janice pulled up beside Valerie's car and parked. She focused her gaze on Valerie, listening intently.

"I . . ." Valerie averted her eyes. "I tried to say no, but Janice, I . . . I hesitated long enough for him to say he would give me time to think about it." She felt the tears she'd been fighting all evening rising to her eyes again. "I'm so ashamed," Valerie confided. "I have to turn him down, but part of me is convinced I will be throwing away happiness."

"Until you realize that the happiness would be fleeting," Janice said, looking at Valerie with a stern compassion in her eyes and voice. "Valerie, sin always looks good, but it ends in destruction. I think you should pay attention to what God is presenting to you in this conference and stop looking at the package Satan is presenting to you."

Valerie looked at Janice. "I know," she said, a slight whimper in her voice, "but—"

There was an urgency to Janice's voice as she squeezed her friend's arm. "But nothing, Valerie. It's time to stop kidding yourself. Stop acting like a giggling teenager swooning over the high school quarterback and pay attention to what Satan is trying to do to you and your marriage. I'm your friend, and I'll be your friend whatever you decide to do. I know that you might not speak to me again after this. But I am going to be honest with you."

There were tears in Janice's eyes. "I have some questions for you. You don't have to answer these for me, but you and God need to talk about them before you move any further with Curtis."

Janice looked out the windshield at the empty parking lot. "Valerie, do you think all of the problems in your marriage are only John's fault?" Janice shook her head sadly. "Why would God, the God who made marriage and gave you a man like John, bring another man into your life for romantic reasons while you are married? Why would God condone your becoming emotionally intimate with another man? Why would God set up an easy way out of a marriage He gave you? How would your being with Curtis honor God? How would you explain your new relationship to your family and friends?"

It was clearly painful for Janice to bring up these questions, but she continued, speaking rapidly as though slowing down might cause her to lose her courage. "Valerie, what kind of Christian man pursues a married woman? What kind of Christian man would try to end a God-ordained marriage?"

Valerie opened her mouth to protest that maybe her marriage had been a mistake, but Janice raised a hand and shook her head. "Hear me out, Valerie. What do you really know about this man, and is he really the kind of man you'd like to be with, knowing that he approached you during a weak time in your life and manipulated your own discontent and sinful desires to destroy your life and benefit him? What would prevent him from doing the same thing with some other woman once you were together and things got rough?"

Valerie was stunned into silence. She'd been so focused on her fantasies about Curtis, she hadn't really thought about what would happen if the Curtis she daydreamed about became the man she needed to relate to on a daily basis.

"You see, Valerie, the only reason this affair has gone on so long—and that's exactly what it is, an affair—is because part of you has wanted it to. The fact is, you don't ever have to talk to Curtis again if you don't want to. You don't have to call him, you don't have to meet him anywhere, you don't ever have to see him again. And I honestly hope you'll think about that. Because if you let this destroy your marriage, Valerie, I'll be here to help you pick up the pieces." She paused and unlocked her door, signaling that it was time for Valerie to go home. "But you know the truth, and you can only blame yourself if you choose not to live by it."

Valerie could see the tears glistening on her friend's cheeks.

"Because you do have a choice."

Twelve

DIFFICULT FRUIT

Valerie was still reeling from her conversation with Janice when Saturday came around. Curtis hadn't called her by then, and she was relieved. Part of her hoped that he had forgotten or given up. Another part was afraid he had.

Still discouraged by her suspicion that her husband was cheating on her, she dragged herself to the last session of marriage seminars.

"I need you to be patient with me while I get my thoughts together," Dr. Matthews said haltingly, sounding uncharacteristically unprepared for the session. He fumbled with his papers and looked offstage distractedly.

John slipped into the seat next to Valerie as Dr. Matthews continued to shuffle the papers on the podium. "It looks like our speaker is having a problem," John whispered. One of the church pianists slid onto the piano bench and began playing a praise song, indicating he wanted the audience to join in. They clapped and sang, wondering when their speaker would come to himself.

Valerie leaned toward John. "I wonder what caused him to forget. He's done these seminars all over the country. He must have gotten some bad news or something." The music didn't seem to bolster him. Gone was the impish grin they'd seen before. "Wonder what we're going to do?"

Dr. Matthews gave a slight nod of his head and ushers Valerie hadn't noticed standing at the end of some of the rows passed down handouts. "Thank you for bearing with me during my moment of confusion," Dr. Matthews said. "Turn to page two."

When Valerie did, the word *patience* seemed to jump off the page in big bold block letters. She looked up to find Dr. Matthews standing at the edge of the podium smiling. He actually began to chuckle. The audience laughed as they realized what he had done.

Laughing, Dr. Matthews walked back to the pianist, grabbed his shoulders, and hugged him.

"Your pastor told me there were Christians in here!" he said, walking toward the audience. "And I see he was right. You have suffered long with me. You've just shown me patience. I could feel it. You felt compassion for me. I thank you."

He paused. "That little bit of playacting demonstrated the patience you should be showing toward your mate. He or she deserves the same compassion, the same patience."

Dr. Matthews clutched his fists together on his chest as if his heart were breaking, as if he were in pain. "A lot of the hurt in relationships, a lot of anguish can be avoided, if one or both of the partners would just exercise a little patience."

Valerie glanced at John. How would their marriage be different if she'd been more patient with him? If she'd shared her concerns with him and given their marriage time to work through its problems instead of turning to another man? *Still,* Valerie thought, *how little patience John has when it concerns me.* She shook her head and wondered if there was any seminar, any speaker, any counselor, anything that could save their marriage. Did she have the patience to work things out, or would it be better to start over—with or without Curtis in the picture?

"Here's how it works," Dr. Matthews continued. "Patience is what we display when we endure difficult circumstances. Think about the patience and longsuffering our God shows to us, time after time," he smiled. "He's our ultimate example of patience and longsuffering. We practice longsuffering when we endure difficult people. Now, all of you were willing to suffer long with me, a stranger. But wives, husbands, have you suffered long with each other?"

Valerie knew she hadn't suffered long with John. And although she'd been willing to try a few weeks ago, she couldn't decide if she still wanted to.

❀ ❀ ❀

"I saved two of the most difficult fruits for last," Dr. Matthews said, leaning against the podium. "I knew if I started with them the first week, none of you would come back," he chuckled. "So now that I have you captive, let's tackle the two tough ones."

"Let's start with faithfulness," he said. "Now, I don't see any reason to hold back here. I've got two major points to share related to this very important fruit of the Spirit. It's a sign of God's work in your life and His presence in your marriage."

"First of all, and most importantly, faithfulness doesn't apply only to your actions. It's a matter of the heart." Valerie felt pained, and hoped it didn't show on her face. "You see, just because you haven't had a sexual relationship with another person, that doesn't mean you've been faithful to your spouse," Dr. Matthews continued. "As a matter of fact, it's fully possible to be unfaithful to your spouse without even being involved with another person, by living in ways that are unfaithful to what God intended for marriage."

Valerie's hands were knotted tightly in her lap. Her involvement with Curtis was proof that her heart had already left John. But as Dr. Matthews pointed out, she'd also been unfaithful to God. She shook her head sadly. She knew what

God had instructed her to do as a wife. Their pastor had preached about it, the ladies' group had conducted its own conference about it, and she'd attended other seminars on being a godly wife. Yet she had chosen to ignore all of that. She'd chosen to see Curtis as some kind of "God-sent deliverer," when she knew she'd been making excuses for her unfaithfulness.

"The hallmark of any good marriage is the couple's faithfulness to each other," Dr. Matthews continued. "Affairs occur because the marriage partner having the affair is looking for something he or she feels is missing in his or her marriage. Oddly enough, the perceived need is not always sexual. But usually the affair is."

He was pacing now. "I want to talk very seriously with you right now. There are some of you here who believe that for whatever reason, you married the wrong person—and have prayed to be free to marry someone else." He stopped pacing and stood silently, letting the audience absorb what he'd said. When he spoke again, he shattered any remnants of Valerie's belief that God wanted her marriage to end.

Valerie felt uncovered. "First and foremost . . . God is never going to say yes to a prayer that goes against His will. In this case, His direct will. Your answer is NO!"

Dr. Matthews looked at the audience and shook his head no. Valerie knew she should never see Curtis again.

"When you think of faithfulness in your marriage, consider your supreme example. Our Heavenly Father has been better than faithful to each of us. His faithfulness endures, never fails, never stops. Since God is the epitome of faithfulness, why would He approve of unfaithfulness in His children? How could He condone it? The answer is, He can't. And don't fool yourselves. God won't bless adultery, whether it takes place in your mind or in someone else's bed. He expects your faithfulness to your relationship with your spouse to overflow. It can, if you follow His leading."

"Now, about self-control," Dr. Matthews said after giving

the group a short break. "Picture this. You and your mate are having a difference of opinion and things are getting rather heated. In that instance, at that moment in time, what do you do? What do you say?"

He began to pace back and forth as though pondering the problem. "First, consider the spiritual realm of this fight." He smiled mischievously. "You are getting all kinds of help. Some of it is good help; some of it is bad help. You've got to look beyond the person you're having a shouting match with and look for your real adversary. One of the angels of darkness is present ringside and his job is to make you lose control. He wants one of you—preferably both of you—to forget all this fruit of the Spirit stuff and really lose it."

Dr. Matthews' voice took on a warning tone. "Whenever you focus on winning an argument instead of solving a problem, whenever you try to hurt your spouse by dredging up things from the past, you lose your focus—working together to defeat the enemy—and start wounding your battle partner, your teammate."

Valerie lowered her eyes. She wondered if she could break her habit of "fighting dirty" whenever she and John disagreed. She wondered if he would bring up her affair whenever they fought if she confessed it to him in its full extent.

"Self-control," Dr. Matthews said, "does not merely involve controlling your tongue or your body. It means taking captive your actions, your attitude, even your thoughts." He paused and allowed his steady gaze to fall on his hearers. "It's difficult to master because it requires a person to be selfless, which is a difficult and sometimes nonexistent concept in America today. But nowhere is self-control needed more than in marriage. That is where what you say or do can hurt another person deeply."

Dr. Matthews stood behind the lectern, picked up his Bible and held it out as if asking the audience to take it. "God loves your marriage. Bring self-control into your marriage to honor Him." He laid down the Bible and asked the group to agree with him in what he would say next. "That means no more backbiting, verbal sparring, tongue-lashings, or having to get in the last word. Okay?" He looked left and right and repeated his question. "Okay?"

He leaned against the side of the lectern, one foot crossed over the other. "You know, it's all right to admit it when you're wrong—because believe it or not, sometimes you are. At the same time, it's a good idea to control your tongue even when you are right. Did you know that? The harmony and peace that will result are made in heaven."

At the break before the final session, Valerie and Janice decided to take a stroll outside where they could have a little privacy to talk. Janice was still interested in how Valerie planned to respond to Curtis.

"I know what I will say," Valerie told her. "I just don't know how I will say it. Curtis is very nice and had really been trying to help me out of a bad situation. I felt like God sent him for a reason."

"Do you really believe God sent Curtis to you? Or that He simply allowed him to pass through your life, but you and Curtis decided to make more of it?" Janice mused. "In any case, I see his entrance into your life as a temptation, and this seminar happening at this time as God's way out."

She paused. "Think about it, Valerie. God knew Curtis was going to be tempted by Satan to return and try one more time to convince you to leave John. In steps one of the most renowned speakers on marriage in the country, conducting a conference on the Fruit of the Spirit. I see God's hand all over this."

"I do too," Valerie said. "You know, Janice, I've felt that way since the beginning of this conference. I know other people are being helped, but I believe God planned it for me. I know that I'm at a point of decision," she confessed, "but I'm just not completely sure what I'll decide."

Janice was silent for a moment. "What you have to ask

yourself, Valerie, is would God send someone to break up your marriage." Janice shook her head. "No, Valerie, God is far from this Curtis episode. I'm praying that you'll be able to see that for yourself before it's too late. And remember that John's been in these sessions the past three weekends with you," she added.

They started back, but before they reached the door, Janice stopped to say what had obviously been on her mind for some time.

"When you first told me about Curtis, I thought then what I'm going to tell you now. After this week, I am convinced I'm right." She took her friend's hand and squeezed it. "Valerie, John loves you. He has proved it to me this week, taking notes and listening to every word. He wants to learn what to do to save his marriage. After this seminar, things should begin to change for you. Pray for God to direct your steps. When you do, letting go of Curtis will be easy."

They returned to their seats. John was already back, and Valerie touched his arm lightly as she sat down. She wondered if he was really sincere, or if he was just playing to the public. Or maybe, like her, he was struggling with a decision about whether he still wanted to stay in their marriage.

Dr. Matthews walked to the edge of the podium to begin the wrap-up session. "God, in His infinite wisdom, has given you His plan for a successful marriage. It's a simple plan. Each and every one of us has traits, characteristics, mannerisms that can, at times, vex our mates." He deliberately overemphasized his words as he said, "Let me put it another way. We can get on each other's nerves." He peered over the top of his glasses like a professor looking at a class of students to see if they had gotten the point he was making, pausing as several members of the audience chuckled.

"But God gave you your mate." He raised his hand as if silencing a crowd—and many were whispering—and said, "I know what you're thinking. I know some of you made your own selection and forgot to ask God. But believe me, God is in the mix. Nobody . . . knows you better than God. He knows every one of your imperfections."

Dr. Matthews walked back and forth, allowing the message to sink in during the silence. "God took your imperfections, found you a mate who needed to develop in a particular area—and your imperfection would help in that development—then He put you together." He closed his hands firmly and ground them together to demonstrate the closeness and the friction. "God is growing you. He is into the growth and development business."

He smiled. "You cannot serve God like you should without getting rid of some of your quirks—your imperfections. One of the ways God forces you to outgrow some of these things is through your relationship with your mate! You may think you are adapting to your partner, but you're actually growing in grace. You see, God has plans for you, plans that require your growth. God is developing you."

"Galatians 5:22 and 23 have given you new freedom—freedom to love your mate God's way," Dr. Matthews said. "Take hold of the power of the fruit," he said. He looked down at us, allowing what he was saying to sink in. "Then," he continued, "enjoy an emotional and physical reunion with your mate unlike any you can ask or think."

As John and Valerie gathered their Bibles and walked to their separate cars to head home, Valerie wondered if John's attitude toward her had changed. She wondered if the sessions they'd attended over the last three weeks would be enough to save their marriage. She sensed that they were more of a starting point than an end. They had a lot of work to do.

But am I willing? Valerie wondered as she pulled out of the parking lot and onto the main road. *And would it be worth it?*

Thirteen

A Costly Choice

Valerie and John arrived home within seconds of one another, still feeling the energy of the conference and the challenges that Dr. Matthews had presented.

John was unusually conversational. "That was really powerful," he said, opening the door for Valerie. "There's no other way to describe it. Dr. Matthews had a lot to say."

He turned to her and smiled tentatively. "He showed me that we have a lot of work to do."

Valerie was surprised. "Yes, we do," she agreed, "but his own testimony is amazing. If his marriage is any indication, well, maybe there's some hope for us."

John's eyes searched Valerie's face. "We'll have to see about that," he said, a note of hope entering his voice.

The look in his eyes—was it interest? Desire, maybe? Valerie found her eyes wandering to the outline of her husband's broad shoulders, visible and attractive in his silk polo. He was a well-built man. She blushed as he noticed her perusal and raised an eyebrow.

"Valerie—" his sentence was interrupted as the telephone rang. Valerie jumped. "I'll get that," she said, brushing abruptly past her husband to slip into the kitchen and grab the phone. "That's probably Janice."

"Hello," she said breathlessly.

"Hello yourself," Curtis replied, his voice teasing and playful. "A little out of breath, I see," he said smoothly.

"Oh . . . we just returned from the conference, and I had to run for the telephone," Valerie explained, conscious of John standing behind her in the kitchen.

"How—How are you doing?" she stammered, fighting her nervousness. Could John tell what was going on?

"I'm just hanging around waiting for a pretty damsel to deliver me from my distress." He laughed. Suddenly, the playfulness in his tone was gone. "Have you thought about it?"

She couldn't answer. She hoped she could silently convey that it wasn't a good time to talk. Not now, not ever.

"Valerie." He drew out her name. "I think about you all the time. I've thought of nothing, of no one else since I let you slip away in April."

Another pause.

"When can I see you?"

Valerie knew she had to say something to get off the phone without giving the impression that she didn't want John to hear what she was saying. "I'll tell you what. I'll research my notes from the staff meeting. Even though it's the weekend, you can call me here tomorrow and I can tell you then, and maybe bring them to you."

Curtis caught on.

"Oh . . . you're not alone. I'll call you tomorrow. In the meantime, I'll think about you all night."

Valerie hung up the telephone and tried to regain her composure. *Oh, please don't let John ask who that was,* she thought. *I think I've lied enough over the last few months.*

She saw the unasked question on her husband's face. He didn't ask who had been on the phone, but he didn't seem interested in their conversation anymore.

"I think I will eat a little something and go to bed," he

said, eyeing her warily. "I have to make a trip to the Hampton Parks store tomorrow." Formality replaced the warmth in his voice. "Goodnight, Valerie."

"Oh," Valerie said, hoping to pick up their conversation. "I wanted to hear some more on what you thought about the couple's conference and Dr. Matthews."

"Don't you have some *research* to do for *someone* who's going to check with you *tomorrow?*" John said pointedly, raising an eyebrow.

"You're right," Valerie said, feeling dejected. "I almost forgot." John's manner dismissed her, and she retreated to her bedroom. John stood in the kitchen, watching her walk away. When Valerie reached the door of their bedroom, she turned around and noticed John studying the caller ID.

※　※　※

Curtis called early the next morning.

"Valerie," he said, enjoying the sound of her sleep-heavy voice. "Where can you meet me for lunch today? Why don't you meet me in the restaurant here for lunch?"

Common sense told her to hang up the phone. To rein in her flesh. To tell him that she didn't want him to call her anymore. To figure out how she could make things right with her husband. She paused, and the opening was enough for Curtis to move the conversation along.

"Valerie, what do I have to do to get you to follow your heart?" he said, cajoling her. "Listen, they have lots of windows, so we will definitely look innocent," his voice took on the patient, coaxing tone one uses with a small child. "We can even sit on the patio area, in full view of everyone."

Valerie took out a pen and asked for the address of the hotel.

※　※　※

The Any Season restaurant was light and airy, yet comfortable and cozy—an excellent meeting place for two friends who had nothing to hide, Valerie thought. *An excellent rendezvous spot if Curtis and I were lovers someday*, she thought, climbing the tile steps leading to the restaurant's exterior entrance.

Curtis sat smiling in the patio area. As she walked toward him, he rose from his chair and winked at the hostess who was rushing to seat her. "I'll get this one," he said.

"Stop," Valerie said playfully. "You're going to make her think I'm trying to be some kind of queen."

Curtis leaned over Valerie as he slid her chair up to the table. "You are some kind of queen," he whispered in her ear, his breath brushing her neck lightly. "You're my queen." He seated himself across from Valerie and took a long look at her.

"What would you like to eat?" His voice was asking a question, but it was not the same question his eyes were asking.

Valerie scanned the menu nervously. "Something light and tasty." She shifted in her chair. "I'll have the Quiche Lorraine and a tall lemonade," she told the waiter. Curtis ordered the salmon, and the waiter brought their drinks before leaving to give the cook their lunch orders.

"You made up your mind quickly," Curtis said, smiling. "You wouldn't be in a hurry, now would you?"

Suddenly Valerie realized what she'd failed to notice before: Curtis was *enjoying* her discomfort. She remembered the look in his eyes when he'd almost kissed her the day she'd tried to break things off with him. It was like he enjoyed the game for the sake of the game. What would he actually do if he won her, the prize? She was risking her marriage, her reputation, her spiritual life, to be with someone who didn't seem to recognize everything she had to lose. Calling her at home the way he had!

Valerie remembered the questions Janice had lovingly

posed to her. What kind of man was Curtis, anyway? Was what she was risking to be with Curtis worth what she was about to throw away by neglecting John?

Valerie looked at the man sitting across from her. He was saying something about happiness and second chances, those long, gorgeous lashes shielding his grey-green eyes. He was one of the most attractive men she had ever seen. Even there in the restaurant he drew stares and second looks, especially from a couple of women two tables over.

But something about him seemed ugly to Valerie now. The soft, full lips she had dreamed of feeling on her own seemed pouty, weak somehow. His persuasive manner suddenly seemed manipulative. She flushed with anger, realizing that Curtis had preyed on her. And with her dying marriage and double-mindedness, she'd been an easy target. She felt her resolve growing. Valerie felt strength flowing through her body, through her heart. She knew what she would do.

"We could have worked out the details," Curtis was saying, oblivious to the change in the woman across from him.

Their orders came, but Valerie was simply moving her quiche around on her plate, praying for strength and formulating the words she would say.

Curtis continued to talk about their future together. His eyes probed her every expression like a laser beam. And although he saw her, he still didn't sense that the Valerie who'd walked in—weak, indecisive, waffling—was suddenly full of resolve.

"My apartment has a pond right outside my bedroom window. We can sit on the terrace in the evenings and . . ." Curtis fell silent. "Looks like I'm going to be sitting on that terrace by myself." His voice was sad but not angry. His eyes looked deeply into her own, finally recognizing what Valerie had realized minutes earlier.

"I'm sorry, Curtis," Valerie said. "This can't go any further.

I am being disloyal to my husband—the man God gave me, the man I vowed to share my life with— by being here with you."

He opened his mouth to protest, but she raised a hand to stop him. "No. *No*. I don't know why it's taken me so long to see what's going on here. Curtis, our relationship would not be blessed. God does not bless adultery, and that's what this is, whether we ever sleep together or not."

She looked for her purse and found her wallet.

"God has set up roadblock after roadblock to these interactions, yet I chose to ignore them," she said, counting out enough bills to pay her share of the check. "I don't really know who you are, Curtis. I know very little about you, except that you were willing to try to lead an unhappy woman out of her marriage. I saw what was going on, yet I was willing to ignore it. Well, I can't ignore it anymore. I'm ashamed of myself."

She placed the bills on the table, and then stood. "I'm sorry. I've been wasting your time, Curtis. I'm going to go home now. Home to work on my marriage. Home to confess to my husband and to try to make things right, if it's not too late," she said, shaking her head sadly. "I wish you the best, Curtis, but I do not want to have any more contact with you."

Curtis seemed stunned.

"Valerie," he said urgently, "you drive a gray car, don't you?"

Surprised by his question, Valerie nodded her head. "What color is your other car?"

"John's car is black, but I seldom drive it."

"A Volvo?" he asked. Valerie nodded. Thinking that Curtis was trying to steer the conversation toward some convoluted illustration, she turned to leave.

"Don't turn around," he said urgently.

"Is John out there?" Valerie asked incredulously. She simply could not believe it.

Curtis was abrupt when he warned her this time. "Don't turn around," he said again. "He has been there watching us for some time now."

Valerie felt a wave of panic sweep over her, but she willed herself to pull it together.

"Goodbye, Curtis," Valerie said, walking briskly toward the door. She didn't look back.

When she reached the parking lot, John's car was gone.

Fourteen

A TIME OF RECKONING

Valerie paced nervously in front of the couch, wringing her hands together. She'd jumped into the car and sped home as soon as she realized what her husband had seen. She shook her head and bit her lip, trying desperately to think of words to explain herself. She felt trapped and guilty.

I should never have gone to see Curtis, Valerie thought ruefully. *Have I ruined my chances with John by meeting Curtis that one last time?*

She felt an odd sense of relief as she heard the garage door open. Maybe John would give her the chance to come clean with him. And this time, she determined, she would not try to hide her guilt from her husband. If the two of them were going to try to rebuild their marriage, she owed him the chance to know the truth. *God,* she prayed, as she heard John's key turn in the lock, *I've really messed things up. I'm so sorry. Please, please don't let it be too late.*

John marched into the house and strode directly toward the kitchen. His eyes focused straight ahead, he seemed determined to ignore his wife.

"John—" Valerie said, stepping behind him as he passed her in the living room. She touched his arm and he shook off her touch, shaking his head as if trying to rid himself of the pleading tone in her voice.

John stopped as he reached the kitchen and opened the cabinet. In the tense silence that hung between them, he chose a glass and poured himself some water from the refrigerator.

A full three minutes passed as he deliberately sipped one, then two full glasses of water before turning to face his wife. Valerie could see a vein throbbing in his neck and knew John was barely holding his composure.

"I want to talk to you," he said in measured tones. Valerie followed him into the family room and stood by a chair. She swallowed, holding back her fear that he was going to ask her for a divorce. How ironic would it be if her husband told her he was leaving her, just as she had finally closed the door on Curtis?

John eyed Valerie warily. "You can sit down," he said, gesturing toward the couch. "You still live here," he laughed, voice dripping with sarcasm.

A muscle twitched rapidly in his jaw.

"I saw you at lunch today," John said, wasting no time in getting to the point. "Want to tell me what's going on?"

"Actually, nothing . . . is going on," Valerie said haltingly. John raised an eyebrow. "Nothing is going on anymore," she clarified. She knew that if she was serious about saving her marriage, she'd better come clean.

John shook his head in disbelief. "Then why the big cover-up last night? What was all that talk about going over something from your office? Do you think I am so stupid that I didn't realize you were lying?" A short, angry laugh escaped his lips.

Valerie met John's eyes and felt the full, withering force of his anger. "I'm sorry, John. Curtis was going back to where he lives, and he offered to treat me to lunch. I accepted against my better judgment, because I'd told him before that I didn't want to see him—" she faltered, and John squinted suspiciously— "I didn't want to see him anymore. But John, I told him today that this was absolutely the end, and I never want to have any contact with him again."

She shook her head ruefully. "I'm sorry, John. I'm so sorry. I shouldn't have gone today. I was discouraged—"

"You shouldn't have gone today," he said, repeating her last words. "You shouldn't have gone *today*." He smirked. "And what about your visits to the park every Saturday?"

Valerie lowered her eyes and winced as though reacting to a blow. He knew! She couldn't believe it. She thought she and Curtis had been discreet. How would John have found out—and how much did he know? Her mind searched frantically for the answers.

John supplied the answer as if reading her thoughts.

"I knew something was up months ago when I went to the park looking for you and ran into Frank," he said, smiling with satisfaction at her discomfort. "He told me that he had seen you and a *friend*, holding hands and walking toward the mall."

Valerie shook her head. So there'd been a reason for Frank's questioning tone at Sandra's home that evening months earlier. He'd seen them. She should have known. Frank would have been more than happy to share what he'd seen.

"But really, Val, I would have suspected even without Frank telling me. I mean, come on," he said, enjoying his response to her revelation. "You left the house around the same time every Saturday with something to read, but you always came back well after dark," he said. "And since when does a woman who hates to dress up unless she has to wear silk pantsuits and perfume to sit on a park bench?"

He was pacing now.

"Let's just get one thing straight. You may refuse to sleep with me. But as long as I am your husband—and I *am* your husband—you will respect me. I thought I made that clear to your friend at the Johnsons' party."

Valerie gasped. John looked at her again. "What did you

think I said to him? I told him exactly what I am telling you—you are my wife. If he felt he could not respect the fact that you are a married woman, he would have to deal with me. I was very serious about that."

"John, I—I'm serious about our marriage too," Valerie said, jumping in as her husband paused to take a breath. "I know it didn't look like it today—and it probably hasn't seemed that way for a while. But haven't you noticed the change in me?"

John wasn't ready for the conflict to de-escalate. "Where does he live?" he said, ignoring her comments.

"Seattle," Valerie answered. She couldn't tell whether or not he was satisfied with her answer, but she decided to press ahead. "John, my relationship with Curtis was wrong. I see that now. But I want you to know that we never even came close to—"

He cut her off. "You know, you and I are supposed to be working on our marriage. Your little lunchtime meeting kind of placed that in jeopardy, don't you think?"

"You're right, John. It was a stupid risk to take. But I do want to work on our marriage, and I do want us to be happy together again. That's why I was so excited about the seminars we went to. I went there hoping I could find a way to keep this marriage together."

"Cutting out your extracurricular lovers would help," he snarled.

"John," Valerie said softly, trying again to explain herself. "My relationship with Curtis was inappropriate. But I want you to know that we weren't involved physically." She didn't know whether it would help the situation, but if they were going to get everything on the table, she figured she might as well share her fears with him.

"I was discouraged today because I've been wondering—" she paused, then decided to forge ahead. "John, are you involved with someone?"

Her words struck a nerve. John was clearly livid. But

whether it was because she was right or wrong, Valerie couldn't tell. He glared at her.

"Don't accuse me, Val. I didn't stop sleeping with you. You made this marriage what it is. You must have wanted me to sleep with someone else. You made sure I stayed away from you. Do you know how that makes me feel?"

Valerie flushed, still feeling the pain of his rejection the night she'd gone to his bedroom. He hadn't acknowledged her at all. She realized afresh that he'd felt the same rejection from her.

"John," she said, her voice a whisper as tears came to her eyes, "John, you didn't even touch me that night when I came to you."

He steeled himself against her tears and shook his head as if he suspected that his wife was trying to manipulate his emotions by crying.

"Oh, I wasn't about to fall into that trap," John said, smiling ruefully and stroking his mustache. His brown eyes flickered with pain and wounded pride. "Oh, you were tempting. But I was not going back to that every other week setup that you proposed. And I'm not some animal who will just perform on command," he spat the words out. "I do have my pride."

"John, I'm sorry," Valerie said, turning to her husband. "I'm sorry. I was thinking only about my own needs. My own pain," she said, willing him to understand. Her voice dropped to a whisper. "I've wanted God to bless us with a baby so much that I've neglected the blessing of our marriage. I took it for granted, and I've taken you for granted, and I'm sorry."

She crossed the room, wringing her hands, then turned to him again, an earnest look in her eyes. "I'm committed to our marriage, John. Committed to God, and to you. I haven't been as committed as I should have been, but I'm committed now."

John looked at Valerie a long moment. "Strangely enough,

I believe you," he said, studying her face. "What other reason would you have had for attending the conference?"

"What was yours?" she said, cocking her head to one side.

"The same. This marriage needs all the help it can get, and I'm also committed to the marriage and to obeying God. Those are the two reasons I stay."

"Janice said you love me, and that's why you stay," Valerie ventured.

John turned and walked toward the kitchen." When is your friend coming back?" he said, facing his wife, a challenge in his eyes.

Valerie shook her head. "I don't think he'll be back, John. I told him today that I was wrong to spend time with him, and that I was choosing to concentrate on my marriage."

She realized that she was hoping he'd take her in his arms and make up for lost time. But John's words signaled the end of their conversation.

"Good. See that you do." He turned and walked to his bedroom.

Fifteen

UNFINISHED BUSINESS

Valerie adjusted her hat for the umpteenth time and shifted positions in the pew at church as Rev. Collins' sermon droned on. She'd been praying that God would speak to her about some more practical ways she could renew her relationship with John, but for the past several Sundays, the sermons seemed to rehash things she already knew well.

Today felt like more of the same. And as the summer heat filled the sanctuary, she realized that she was bored and hot. Looking at John, she breathed a silent prayer of frustration, once again asking God for a practical word from the sermon. She motioned to the usher for a fan, then crossed her legs and fanned herself, causing her short auburn curls to flutter slightly around her face.

John turned from his Bible and glanced at her, his annoyance at her fidgeting clear. She sighed and tried to refocus on the message.

"Now, I'd like you to turn to 1 Corinthians 11:26–27," Rev. Collins said. Relieved to have something to do, Valerie paged quickly to the passage and followed along as Rev. Collins read aloud: "'For whenever you eat this bread and drink this cup, you proclaim the Lord's death until he comes.

Therefore, whoever eats the bread or drinks the cup of the
Lord in an unworthy manner will be guilty of sinning against
the body and blood of the Lord.'

"We read this passage whenever we prepare for Communion," Rev. Collins said, motioning for the deacons to get
ready to serve the Lord's Supper. "But I'm concerned that we
don't always take it as seriously as we should. You see, Paul
was trying to tell the Corinthians that when they took the
Lord's Supper without examining their hearts for uncon-
fessed sin, they missed the true purpose of this sacrament—
honoring Christ's sacrifice for us on the Cross. In fact, they
were actually dishonoring that sacrifice and sinning against
the One who provided it."

Rev. Collins paused and looked across the congregation.
"Now, we don't always do this. But I'd like us to spend the
next few moments before we share the Lord's Supper examining our hearts." He walked slowly across the stage. "Think
carefully about the way you've lived since the last time you
took Communion," he said. "Is there a sinful pattern in your
life that you haven't repented of? Are you in conflict with a
Christian brother or sister? Do you need to mend brokenness
in your relationship with God, or with someone in your life?"

He motioned for the organist to play. "We're going to
spend some time in silent prayer. I'd like to encourage you to
ask God to show you if there is unresolved business that you
need to take care of in order to celebrate His death and resur-
rection with honesty and reverence. We need to accept this
special meal with brokenness in our hearts over our sin—and
with joy and gratitude for His sacrifice, which cleanses our
souls."

He bowed his head and prayed silently for a few minutes. As the congregation joined him, Valerie asked God to
reveal the areas of her life that needed work, the sins that
needed to be confessed.

Valerie wasn't prepared for the onslaught of images that
filled her thoughts. Her mind's eye replayed scenes of

Valerie refusing to show her husband small kindnesses, of her choosing to neglect her marriage, of her sending John away and denying his needs. She saw herself in the mall, lingering over baby clothes and allowing her deep sorrow over the miscarriage to become a seething rage she focused on John. She realized that her God-given desire to mother a child had become an idol that she'd worshiped instead of acknowledging the good things God had given her and finding constructive ways to deal with her pain. She saw herself pouring out her heart to Curtis instead of trying to explain her grief to John. Tears came to her eyes as Rev. Collins' voice floated over the speakers throughout the church.

"God is speaking to many of your hearts today," he said softly, compassion in his voice. "It's clear that He's showing many of you that you have some unfinished business to deal with, in your relationship with Him and in your relationships with one another." He paused. "In fact, some of you are realizing that you shouldn't take Communion today without resolving the things the Holy Spirit has shown you."

Valerie squeezed her hands together, grateful that everyone's eyes were still closed. That way, no one could sense her discomfort.

"Here's what we are going to do today," Rev. Collins continued. "I know that we usually pass the bread and wine down the rows to one another. But we're going to do something different this Sunday," he said. "Row by row, the ushers are going to lead you to the altar. The deacons and I will serve Communion to those who feel comfortable taking it. But if God has shown you something in your life that you need His help resolving, why don't you spend a few moments here at the altar, praying for the strength and forgiveness that He promises us."

Valerie wondered what people would think if they noticed her praying at the altar instead of taking Communion. Would they suspect that there were problems between her and John?

Rev. Collins seemed to anticipate her fear. He paused, looking over the bowed heads in the crowded sanctuary. "Now the Bible tells us that all of us have sinned. We all fall short of God's glory. Not one of us has any righteousness of our own to offer God. And we know that although Jesus' blood places us in a position of righteousness before God, we are still working out that righteousness in a practical way in our lives." He cleared his throat. "So as we're praying and taking the Lord's Supper here today, I don't want anyone looking around, taking note of who's eating and who's praying. We're doing kingdom business here, being honest before God, and I don't want anyone taking the body and blood for show, afraid of what people will say if you don't. And I don't want anyone refusing the holy meal because of false guilt or fear about what other people think of you. Let's enjoy freedom among one another, and freedom before God." Valerie felt a flood of relief wash over her as Rev. Collins approached the altar and removed the white cloth that covered it. The deacons joined him, slipping on crisp white gloves before handling the gold trays that held the wafers and small cups of grape juice.

When the usher motioned her row to the altar, Valerie was focused on bringing her load of sin and guilt to God. She prayed earnestly for God to restore her relationship with Him, for Him to stop the sinful ways of thinking that had alienated her from God and her husband, despite her best efforts. She rose and returned to her seat, feeling cleansed and strengthened in her desire to make things right with John.

On the drive home, Valerie prayed for the right words to tell her husband what God had revealed to her about her part in damaging their marriage. She realized that God would bless her desire to humble herself before her husband.

"John," she ventured, breaking the silence that hung between them, "I had to confess my sins against you to God instead of taking Communion today."

John glanced at Valerie, his eyes leaving the road briefly. He didn't respond, but Valerie plunged ahead.

"I realized that I was refusing to take responsibility for my own pain," she said, looking ahead at the road before turning to him again. "And instead of sharing how I felt with you, I turned inward and away."

Valerie lowered her voice. "And I . . . denied you, and I tried to control you and punish you instead of working out how I felt with you." She shook her head. "I'm so sorry, John."

Valerie knew she'd caught her husband by surprise, and could sense him trying to decide what he'd say next. His hands tightened on the steering wheel.

"Who did you turn to?" he asked, an accusing note in his voice. "Your musician friend?"

Valerie flinched and felt a wave of shock pass over her. She knew John was right, but she didn't expect him to want to hurt her again—not after she'd bared her soul to him and shared her guilt. She blinked away the tears that rose to her eyes and fought her desire to respond. Fighting back would only cause more friction. And although her first instinct was to fight with John, to argue with the ugly tone he was using, she heard something beyond his anger. She heard the pain in his voice.

Valerie realized that in sharing her pain, she'd told her husband that his response to the miscarriage had let her down somehow. She'd told him that she had needed more support than he'd been able to give. Maybe he'd been hurting too, and hadn't known how to share it with her.

Sitting there in the car, Valerie breathed a silent prayer for the complete restoration of her marriage to John. She prayed for faith, even though her circumstances seemed so bleak and hopeless.

She asked God for the strength to trust Him for a marriage that was more broken than she realized.

❋   ❋   ❋

Later that evening, Valerie dozed lazily on the couch, watching a film and thinking absently about the arrangements she needed to finalize for an upcoming exhibit the next day. She was startled when John walked in the room and stood in front of the television, blocking her view.

She sensed his nervousness and looked up, shifting the pillow she'd been leaning on. John clasped his hands together.

"I'm sorry for what I said in the car," he said gruffly. Valerie nodded. John passed out of the room, and the interchange was over, as quickly as it had begun.

Valerie knew he was sincere and wondered if he had been praying. She felt a twinge of hope.

Still, he didn't move toward her, or come to their bedroom later that night. She wondered whether his apology was the beginning of a healing for their marriage, or if he was committed to someone else. The thought tore at her heart. If he was planning to leave her for someone else, Valerie thought, she could only blame herself.

Sixteen

RENEWING THE NEST

Valerie was awakened Saturday morning as the phone rang impatiently. She glanced groggily at the alarm clock on the night table as she rolled over to answer the phone and was startled to see that it was eleven o'clock. Had she really slept that long?

"Hello?" she said, rubbing the sleep from her eyes. She heard Janice's familiar laugh on the other end.

"Girl, are you still sleeping? It's almost noon. Don't you have anything to do on a Saturday morning? Chores to catch up on, or something?"

Valerie could sense the amusement in her friend's voice and responded with her own chuckle as she leaned back against her pillows.

"You know, I was just exhausted when I got home last night. The museum has a new exhibit opening Monday, and I worked late making sure everything was just so. It was all I could do to wash my face and brush my teeth before I fell into bed," she said, yawning.

"Well, I'm glad I called," Janice said. "Did you forget? We've got a meeting of the planning committee for the Christian women's symposium at church at 12:30."

Valerie sat straight up in bed. "Oh, Janice! I'm glad you called too! I'd completely forgotten about that meeting!" She glanced at the pillows scattered around her and scrambled out of bed. "Now, um, remind me what it is we're talking about at this meeting?" she said, jamming her feet into her slippers and padding toward the kitchen to make herself some toast.

"We're going to decide which speakers we'd like to invite this year," Janice said.

"Oh!" Valerie said, smacking her forehead with the heel of her hand. "I know I was supposed to come up with a few ideas, but I haven't had time to think of anything."

"No problem," Janice said. "Do you remember the speaker from last year?"

Valerie shook her head, almost dropping the phone nestled between her ear and shoulder as she struggled to pour herself a glass of orange juice. She slammed the refrigerator door with her hip and leaned against the island in the middle of the kitchen to sip her juice and try to wake up. "No, but I remember she got a great reception. I heard a lot of good feedback from her sessions."

"She was really good," Janice said. "What I valued most were some of the practical tips she gave us. Just little things, but they helped me in all kinds of ways."

Valerie's curiosity was piqued. "Like how?" she said.

"Well, one of the things I remember most was a special home care session she led," Janice said. "She mentioned the importance of making your home a welcoming place for your husband and family—just taking a little extra care in decorating, keeping things neat, creating a homey atmosphere," she said. "I started making an extra effort to keep things attractive in my house after that. It was hard—Tim and I both work, and we're both exhausted when we get home—but it's really been worth it," Janice continued. "Tim's not sure exactly how I've changed things up, but I have noticed that he's more comfortable at home. Sometimes we just stay home and relax instead of going out on weekends," she said, a smile in her voice.

Valerie was intrigued. "Janice, I think you've inspired me," she said, looking around at the kitchen. "I'll see you at the meeting," she said.

Janice heard something in her friend's voice. "Valerie, what are you up to?" she said. "I can hear the bells and whistles going off in that head of yours."

Valerie grinned. "You'll see," she said, a note of mystery in her tone. "I've got to go!"

Valerie put a couple of slices of bread in the toaster. While they toasted, she walked around the house.

It looked like she'd been feeling—unhappy. Old newspapers were piled beside the sofa. There were several pairs of shoes in the living room, and an open bag of chips languished on the coffee table among several months' worth of magazines and TV guides, its former sheen covered by a thin layer of dust. *The house looks more like a bird's nest than a love nest,* Valerie thought, walking through the rest of the house and observing the clutter and disarray. *How did I let everything slide so? It's no wonder John and I don't spend any time together here.*

She stood in the doorway of her bedroom and surveyed the scene in front of her. When had she stopped cleaning regularly? As she looked with new eyes, Valerie saw the pile of clothes thrown in a chair—clothes she'd been meaning to take to the dry cleaners. The bills and papers she had worked on in the middle of her bed were still there. There was dust on the furniture and the vanity mirrors needed to be cleaned. Jewelry and clothes hung out of partially opened drawers. Books and newspapers covered the floor and the settee at the foot of the bed. And when had the comforter on the bed faded so? How long had the pillows been so flat?

Valerie shook her head ruefully. She'd been too distracted and depressed to realize that this was not the room of a woman trying to encourage her husband to join her there.

Valerie smiled to herself, feeling a surge of energy. The

house was dirty and uninviting now, but it didn't have to stay that way.

"Thank you, Lord," Valerie said. Then she headed to the phone to call Janice. She'd changed her mind. She would just have to miss today's committee meeting.

She had more urgent matters to take care of.

❊ ❊ ❊

Janice gasped appreciatively as she walked into Valerie's new and improved master bedroom.

Valerie smiled. "You like what I've done so far?"

"Like?" Janice tilted her head and grinned at her friend. "Valerie, you've really outdone yourself. When did you get the drapes, and what is going on with this bed set off like this?"

"Well . . ." Valerie said mischievously, "I was looking through some decorating magazines when I got the idea to set the bed off from the rest of the room to make the bedroom into a lovers' paradise." She paused dramatically. "I'm calling it my . . . boudoir."

Janice chuckled. "Girl, are you blushing?"

"I'll be doing more than that, if all goes according to plan," Valerie said saucily, and the two women laughed together.

Janice looked around in awe as Valerie watched, satisfied. After she'd cleaned the rest of her house, Valerie had turned all of her attention to the bedroom. She intended to invite her husband back, and she wanted him to like what he saw. Valerie wanted to surrender herself like a lush, succulent fruit ready to be plucked, and so their bedroom had to be a beautiful place, an irresistible garden. She'd gone after the effect she wanted with gusto.

A low, horizontal glass-enclosed fireplace already served as a divider that created separate sleeping and reading alcoves in the room. Valerie had made the effect more dramatic by enclosing the bed in French draperies that could be pulled back at the entrance to the sleeping space. The beige and rose print drapes matched a new beige coverlet that was accented by rose piping and pillow shams.

"I wanted your opinion because I love how you've decorated your house, Janice," Valerie said. "Do you have any other ideas for me?"

"Do I? I'm about to explode!" Janice said, catching her friend's excitement.

"Don't hold back, then!" Valerie laughed at Janice's obvious pleasure. "I figured we could go shopping this afternoon. I want to finish the bedroom today, and then —" she blushed again—"I'll get myself ready."

Valerie motioned Janice over to one corner of the bedroom and tried to explain just what she wanted to accomplish. "I want to welcome John back to our bedroom—and I want him to feel like it's a place where he can be comfortable." She cleared her throat. "I decided to buy a special dresser for him and put some intimate items in it," Valerie said. "I'm going to use every way I can think of to appeal to his five senses, from the feel of the fabric to the smell of the room."

Janice nodded. "That's a great idea, Valerie. After all, God gave our senses to us so that we could enjoy them—and so that married people could enjoy them together." She smiled and squeezed her friend's arm. "Girl, it is so good to see you taking so much interest in working on your marriage! You've come a long way over the last few months."

Valerie grinned. "Don't stop praying for me, Janice," she said. "I'm looking for romance with pizzazz—and more, I hope."

"I understand, exactly," Janice said. "I'll keep praying."

They started to leave and Janice took one last look at the room. "I had forgotten how beautiful this room is. It's been a long time since I've been in here."

Valerie nodded. It had been a long time since John had

been there too. But she hoped with all her heart that he'd be
back.

※ ※ ※

Valerie had felt inhibited around Janice when her
thoughts had been full of Curtis, but now that she'd rededi-
cated herself to her marriage, she shared freely—hoping her
friend could offer some godly advice.

"Don't worry, Valerie," Janice said, steering her van onto
the highway on-ramp. "I honestly believe that you and John
will recapture the special feeling you had," she said. "I remember how you were. Don't you? John was obsessed with
pleasing you."

"He was, wasn't he?" Valerie sighed. "How can I get
things to go back to the way they were?"

"You start by doing what we just learned," Janice said pa-
tiently. "Have you had any opportunities to really use the
fruit of the Spirit?"

"I decided I could not make the fruit work by trying to
master them all at one time, so I chose kindness," Valerie
replied. "I'm hoping that John will see my invitation and the
work I'm putting into the room as an act of kindness for him.
And I've really been trying to be polite to him, to say 'please'
or 'thank you' or to offer a compliment whenever it seems
appropriate," she said.

Janice smiled. "What a great idea," she said. "Concentrat-
ing on one fruit at a time makes it easier to do."

She pulled into the parking lot at the store, and they
walked to the section where bedroom furnishings were
stocked. Valerie chose the dresser she wanted, and arranged
to have it delivered to her home. Janice went to the accessory
section and selected two huge urns and some silk beige, rose,
and gold stalks to set inside them. She planned for them to
sit near the windows in the reading alcove.

"That's gorgeous!" Valerie exclaimed. "I can't wait to see

John's eyes when he sees our boudoir," she said, shrugging her brows seductively. Janice shook her head and they laughed together.

※　※　※

After their trip to the home furnishings store, the women decided to stop at Cherie's, one of their favorite lunchtime haunts, for dessert. "The pastry here keeps showing up all over me," Janice said, patting her stomach. "You seem to be holding up pretty well."

"I wish," Valerie said. "I have twenty pounds tucked away. It wouldn't hurt to lose a few of them by next week."

Janice nodded. "You really want to surprise John." She smiled. "I understand."

"Oh, Janice, not really. Things had really gotten bad before the conference."

Valerie paused and looked around them. Cherie's was femininity personified, from the lacy curtains on the windows to the ruffled tablecloths around each round table for two. Women came there to chat, to unwind. They sipped raspberry teas laced with orange slices and nibbled ladyfingers or dainty slices of cake. And, for a moment, they weren't wives or mothers or career women or caretakers. They were simply girlfriends, girlfriends who had a few moments to revel in their own femininity and the sweet fellowship of sisters.

Once they had been seated, Valerie plunged in without ceremony. "I . . . haven't been able to share this with anyone," she said, her voice dropping to a whisper. "John—John and I are seldom intimate," she said, her words sounding foreign to her. She averted her eyes, ashamed of her revelation. It hurt that her situation had become so serious.

Janice didn't seem surprised. "I had kind of figured that," she said, reaching across the table to squeeze her friend's hand. "After our talk at the conference, I was pretty sure that was the case. Tell me what happened with you two."

"Oh, Janice," Valerie sighed. "So much of it was my fault."

Janice's eyes reflected her concern. "Valerie, you used to tell me how wonderful John was and how much you needed him. What happened?"

"Janice . . ." Valerie searched for words. "I wish it was something I could explain simply." She toyed with her spoon. "I always assumed when John and I got married that we'd be able to have a family. We started really trying a couple of years ago, and we really struggled. It became a strain between us," she said. "I don't think John really understood how badly I wanted a baby, how much I wanted to be a mother," she said softly. "For a while, the problem wasn't that we weren't being intimate," Valerie laughed ruefully. "We were together all the time! And, unfortunately, it became routine, almost like a chore we had to do. Ironically, we really lost a lot of the emotional intimacy and the closeness that we used to have. I think John probably felt like I had become pretty controlling about that part of our relationship. And each month was just a roller coaster of emotion for me—the hope I felt when I thought maybe I was pregnant, and the awful grief I felt when I discovered I wasn't. Over and over again." She shook her head.

"Finally, after months of trying, I was pregnant!" she said, a smile coming to her lips. "I couldn't believe it! I went shopping for maternity clothes and little baby things the same day I found out. I thought I'd finally have the little one I wanted; finally John and I would have the family we'd dreamed about when we were dating." She stopped and sipped the iced tea their waiter had brought. "But I lost the baby just a few weeks later."

There were tears in her friend's eyes. "Oh, Valerie," Janice said softly.

"I don't think either of us really knew how to deal with losing a child, even a child we hadn't even chosen a name for," Valerie said. "We were grieving a death, feeling an awful disappointment after so much anticipation, so much prayer," she said. "I think in some ways, we probably both felt like failures. After all, aren't our bodies made for having children? And we just couldn't cope."

"I still cry when I think about our little girl. On the day of the month I discovered I was pregnant, on what would have been the baby's due date, even through diaper commercials on television," Valerie said. "I needed to talk to John, I needed him to talk to me about the baby, I needed him to understand how I felt. But he'd turned inward. He really immersed himself in his work.

"When I met Curtis, I thought I'd found the confidant I needed so badly. But I realize—I realize now—that John was hurting just as much as I was, and that working was his way of coping with his pain. We turned away from each other when we needed each other more than ever. For a while, neither of us was interested in being intimate. And when he was, I wanted to control things. I was angry at him for not being able to give me what I needed, and I rejected him." She paused, not knowing if her next words would be too much, even for her friend. "I didn't want him, Janice."

"Don't you feel attracted to him?" Janice probed gently.

Valerie stared out the window they were seated by. "I do now," she said. "But by the time I realized that, I'd stopped sleeping with him. And all of the closeness that we'd shared before our struggle with infertility just evaporated, a little each day, until I came to the point where I almost abandoned my marriage," she said, a note of shame in her voice. "At first I would just tell John 'no.' After that, I told him that more than once every couple of weeks was ridiculous."

"I can imagine that did not go over well with him." There was sympathy in Janice's voice.

"I knew immediately he did not like it. He told me in no uncertain terms what he thought. But things got worse."

Janice took a bite of her sandwich and looked at Valerie. "You're kidding, aren't you? Don't you think that was going too far?"

"At the time, I didn't think it was far enough," Valerie said ruefully.

"What?"

Valerie played with the stirrer in her raspberry tea and tried to think of a polite way to tell Janice just what she'd done to her marriage. "Janice . . . John and I don't sleep in the same bedroom, and all efforts at intimacy have stopped— sexual or otherwise."

Valerie saw the flash of pain cross Janice's face. And she hadn't even told her the worst.

"And when I realized how foolish I was being—or maybe it was that I finally wanted him instead of the other way around—Janice, the tables had turned."

Cheeks flushed with embarrassment, Valerie recounted how she'd been determined to force John to make love to her. She told Janice how she'd shed her clothes for a sheer robe. How she'd approached her husband, inhaling the in- toxicating, familiar scent of his cologne. How he'd ignored her and how she'd lain next to him all night, untouched and sniffling, pride wounded.

"John showed me just how much I had hurt him," she said, hurt in her voice. "When I had refused him, he had to have felt inadequate and humiliated. It hurts me to think about it. But as strange as it seems, I believe John really does love me . . . and he loved me that night. But he's just as stubborn as I am, and he was simply insulating himself against any more pain. I had been so cruel to him, and he gave me a taste of my own medicine."

"How is it now between you, since the conference?" Janice asked.

"Well," Valerie said, toying with the Italian cream cake they were eating. "We still sleep in separate bedrooms, but what I feel for him is just the opposite of what I once felt. You see all that I'm doing now. And Janice, just by putting into practice being kind to him, I can feel a difference, a change. I wonder sometimes if he wants to get back to the way we were too."

Valerie realized again what an awful mistake she'd made by shutting her husband out of her heart and refusing to share herself with John. *Could a simple invitation and a few decorations make amends for years of problems?* she wondered.

Janice tried to encourage her. "Valerie, you've made a lot of strides in the right direction."

"I try to stay encouraged, Janice. And working on this project has really given me hope. But I don't think John is interested anymore. And I know it takes two to damage a marriage, and it will take me, John, and God to repair ours. I just don't know if he's up to it. But honestly, Janice, there's nothing I want more."

Valerie peered longingly through the lacy curtains on the window beside the table. "Janice . . . I want him back," she whispered.

Janice nodded. "We can't stop praying about this, Valerie. Whatever you do, don't stop praying."

"I gave it to God first," Valerie said, nodding in agreement. "I am so scared of getting hurt and rejected, I immediately asked God to order my steps."

"Then you're on the right track," Janice assured her. "I don't think you have to worry."

"You're right. God began working right away. After I prayed about it, I came up with a plan to invite John to a rendezvous on this coming Friday night."

"A rendezvous?" Janice was thrilled. "What a romantic idea."

"There is no way I could have thought of a rendezvous on my own. I really believe the idea came from God," Valerie said. "As soon as I finish making the arrangements, I'm going to write an invitation to him," she smiled with anticipation. "I've been reading through the Song of Solomon for inspiration," she said playfully.

Janice squealed with delight. "Valerie, I don't think you have a thing to fear. John will be there." She smiled knowingly. "So *that's* why there is all the hurry to get the bedroom ready."

"Right," Valerie said. "And now, I've got to get myself ready."

Janice smiled with more confidence than Valerie felt. "Wait on the Lord, Valerie. John will come around. This upcoming rendezvous may be the thing he is waiting on."

"I sure hope so," Valerie said. "I sure hope so."

Seventeen

THE ALLURE

W hat about this one?" The saleswoman said, spritzing a square of paper with yet another perfume before handing it to Valerie.

Valerie took the card and inhaled deeply. "Oh, this one is nice too, Lydia. But I'm not sure it's quite what I need."

Lydia chuckled. "If I may say so, ma'am, this must be a very special occasion you're planning for. You've tried almost every perfume I have!"

Valerie leaned forward confidentially. "I'm planning a special evening with my husband," she said, barely hiding her giggle behind her hand. "Everything has to be just right."

Lydia raised an eyebrow. "It's my pleasure to help," she said. "When I opened this shop, I hoped to help women pamper themselves. It's been a nice benefit to see them pamper their husbands too," she said with a smile. "I'm going to leave you for a moment. I'll let you choose your own perfume, but I do think I've got something in the back room you might like."

Valerie grinned. When she'd first passed the posh boutique on her way home from work a few months ago, she hadn't been the least bit interested in buying anything special to wear to bed. But now, she could hardly choose between all of the silky negligees and other intimate items in Lydia's shop.

Valerie wanted to choose some special items to enjoy with her husband. She wanted to show him that she cared about him, and that she wanted to be intimate just to show her love, without the pressure to conceive a child. So here she was, sniffing perfumes, shower gels, soaps, and moisturizers to find something he'd like.

Just as she found a perfume she liked, Lydia emerged from the back room holding a silky full slip in deep rose. A tiny heart on the bodice accentuated the bust line. Valerie saw her selection and gasped in surprise. "Lydia, it's perfect!" she breathed, setting down a jar of perfume and fingering the lingerie. She held it against her body. "This is it! This is exactly what I want."

She turned and saw a sweet silk robe tucked away on a clearance rack of several items. Lydia laughed aloud as Valerie made a beeline toward a pair of matching slippers.

"What are you laughing about? What have I missed?" Valerie said, sure she had missed something in her excitement at finding all the items she needed in the same shop.

"Oh no, you haven't missed a thing," Lydia said. "I was just looking at the joy on your face." She paused, and Valerie could tell she was considering her next sentence. "I don't usually talk this way to my customers, but I just have to say this. I sense that God is doing something special for you. I believe He's set this day aside for you to find everything you need. He's right on time," she said, shaking her head. "I have to tell you, none of my sales associates had thought about putting together the things you've selected, but what a gorgeous ensemble! God must be really pleased with you."

Valerie glowed. Maybe all of this was a coincidence, but she didn't think so. In some way, it felt like God really was pleased with her. She hoped He would continue to bless her plans.

"I would love to think that," she said, pulling her credit

card from her purse with a flourish.

※　※　※

Valerie sat pensively on her newly decorated bed, her purchases from Lydia's surrounding her. She glanced at the pen in her hand and willed herself to write something, anything on the hand-painted card she'd selected for John.

She'd been so excited about all of her other preparations, but now she was afraid. She tapped the pen against her chin. She wanted her invitation to John to say something special, something inviting, something that made her intentions clear. John had been working even more than usual, and she hadn't been able to talk to him much at all.

But even though it was easier than talking to him, the thought of writing a letter to him filled her with butterflies. Would John acknowledge the letter, or would he ignore it? Would he be completely uninterested? What if he responded cynically, the way he had when she'd confessed to him that Communion Sunday?

She wondered what her friends at work would think about the tactics she was using. She knew they would look down on her for humbling herself this way, for using physical intimacy to reignite her marriage when she needed so much more than sex.

But Valerie was willing to give, and stay in prayer about it, until God saw fit to change John. She was through with locking God out of her bedroom. She'd told the whole awful story to Him, and she honestly believed He'd inspired her plan. She wasn't about to let pride turn her around.

"Oh ye of little faith," Valerie chuckled aloud. She had been praying and praying for a breakthrough, asking God to make all kinds of steps for her and rekindle old fires, yet she became weak-kneed and fearful when it came her turn to act.

She got up and paced the room, speaking aloud to encourage herself. "Why all the preparation and planning, if

I'm just going to retreat before the first shot is even fired?" she told herself. "After all, it's not like I don't know this man. It's not as if we have no history together. This is my husband I'm thinking about."

When she thought back far enough, Valerie could remember happier times. She remembered how she felt when she was working or thinking and John would join her. She remembered how her voice had a lilt when she greeted him, how he knew by her tone and expression how important he was to her. She'd felt the same way when he would call her during his lunch break or when he'd drop by with flowers, just because. Treasured. Special. But somewhere along the line, they'd stopped. They'd stopped caring, and they'd stopped trying. Pleasing each other had lost its importance as they each tried to find ways to deal with their pain.

At first the change showed itself in small ways. A change in tone, a neglected "please, dear" or "thank you." Then, several days would pass between "I love you" or "you're important to me." They had begun to take each other for granted, and forgot their promise to cherish one another. Each put their needs ahead of the other's, and forgot that they were to work together as a team.

Valerie sighed. She knew that the way she'd begun to live was in direct opposition to what God had directed her to do: to be subject to John. She had read it in Colossians, Ephesians and Titus, and she knew she was wrong. God had given her a reason for being subject to John—because it pleased Him.

If only I had seen my marriage as the gift from God that it was, I would never have stopped showing love to my husband, she thought. *I can remember a time when a look was all it took for me to know what John was thinking. He could sense my thoughts sometimes too—he always saw so much more of my heart than anyone else. And now he always seems so far away.*

Now Valerie was nervous about sending John a letter— something she used to do frequently. She remembered when she never wondered what to say. When the words seemed to pour from her fingers. She'd always begun with a "Dearest John." Sometimes they'd exchanged the "Love Note" cartoon from the newspaper. And how many times had she gone to a greeting card shop to get a card for someone, and come out with a number of "just because" cards for John. Back then, doing for him was a joy, and the feedback was wonderful. She'd received as much as she'd given. Maybe more. Tears came to her eyes, and she bowed her head.

"Oh, God, forgive me," she whispered. "Forgive me for my sins, forgive me for my fear. You said in Your word, 'Greater is He that is in you, than He who is in the world.' Lord, I need Your strength to be greater than my fear, Lord, because I'm afraid. I need Your Spirit to give me words that are pleasing and alluring. Lord, I want to take a step in faith to restore my marriage, and I ask You to help me reach my husband in a way that he can't ignore. Lord, I so badly want things to go well on Friday evening. I want my husband back, Lord. I want my marriage back. But, Father, even if things do not happen the way I've planned, I believe Your promise, that all things work together for good for those who love You, and are called according to Your purpose. Help me not to falter or doubt You. I will trust You to work Your wonderful will in my life. Only You know if I am ready to receive Your blessing. I thank You for the words You will give to me. And I thank You for the redeeming blood of Jesus in whose name I pray. Amen."

Then she sat down again and wrote:

Dearest John,

I joyfully invite you to a secret rendezvous in my boudoir, at your home on Friday night. After a lovingly prepared meal, I urge you to take a stroll through your flourishing garden, where all the luxuriant fruit and aromatic blossoms yearn to be plucked only by you. I miss you, John. Please come.

Love,
Valerie

Eighteen

A RENDEZVOUS

Valerie's thoughts were interrupted by the ring of the oven timer. She rushed over to the oven and, grabbing a pair of potholders from the counter, pulled a roasted chicken from the oven. As she inhaled the steam that rose from the seasoned meat, she checked the clock. John would be home within an hour.

It had been a week since she'd left her invitation on the pillows in his bedroom, but things between them hadn't changed. Their home was still quiet, and they still lived more like busy roommates than husband and wife. Valerie sighed, nervous. She didn't know whether or not he planned on joining her for the special evening she'd planned, but she was determined to be prepared if John did come. She opened a pot on the stove and checked the wild rice, then popped a peach cobbler into the oven to warm. She hoped it would make the house smell warm and inviting.

Valerie smiled to herself. She realized yet again that some women—the sassy "sistas" on television sitcoms, the women at work, and probably some of her own close friends—would laugh at the tactics she was using to win her husband back. There'd been a time when she would have

laughed at herself for rushing home from work and scurry-
ing around the kitchen like this in the hopes of luring her
husband to the bedroom. But she honestly felt that God had
inspired her plan. Here was a way to tell her husband, without using words, that she cared about him, that she wanted
him back.

She ran a wet rag over the counter, then ran her fingers
over her glossy auburn curls. Breathing a quick prayer for a
miracle, she rushed to take a shower. She wanted everything
to be just perfect.

⁂　⁂　⁂

Valerie had just slipped the silk robe over her shoulders
and spritzed her body with perfume when she heard John's
key turn in the door. As much as she wanted to rush out to
meet him—or at least to see the look on his face as the scents
of his favorite foods wafted over him—she stopped for one
last prayer.

"Father, if it is Your will, please let our reconciliation
come tonight. And, Lord, if this isn't Your time, give me the
strength I need to be patient and wait on You. Father, give
me the right words to say to keep our conversation going, to
make this a warm evening, and to live what You say in Your
Word. You have done so much, and I thank You, Lord. You
are indeed awesome and gracious. Thank You for hearing my
prayer. Thank You for giving me hope. Thank You in the
powerful name of Jesus. Amen."

Valerie tied the robe at her waist, slipped her feet into
the dainty slippers, and went to greet John. When she made
her way to the door, her husband was standing in the entryway, a look of mild surprise on his face.

"Hi," she said nervously, feeling his eyes sweep over her
appreciatively.

"Hi," he said, her own nervousness mirrored on his face.

Regaining her composure, Valerie took John's briefcase

and gestured for him to join her in the dining room. "How was your day?" she said, handing him a cold lemonade.

As they sipped their lemonade, John began to tell Valerie about some of the issues connected with the chain of restaurants he managed. As she peppered the conversation with questions about his work, Valerie could barely hide her joy. Here they were, truly talking to one another, showing interest in each other's lives, sharing the way they used to.

Thank you, God! she thought.

"It sounds like you had a pretty full day," Valerie said, gently slipping John's lemonade from his hand. "Why don't you shower in the master bath while I finish dinner? There's something in there for you."

John looked at Valerie with a light of interest in his eyes as he rose from the table and walked toward their bedroom.

As soon as he left the kitchen, Valerie dialed Janice's number. She didn't even wait for her friend to say "hello" before she launched into a progress report. "So far, so good!" she whispered. "Are you still praying?"

Janice chuckled on the other end of the line. "Praying, yes, and fasting too," she said. "Matter of fact, I can almost taste that roast chicken over here," she said, a note of playful grouchiness in her voice. "All I know is, you'd better be on your knees for me the next time I need a breakthrough," she teased her friend.

Valerie laughed. "You've got it. With all the praying you've done for me, I owe you big time," she said. She heard the water in the bathroom stop running. "Gotta go."

"Well, remember all the details—'cause I want to hear them tomorrow. I've earned the right!" Janice said as she hung up.

❀ ❀ ❀

Valerie smelled the fresh, masculine scent of the shower gels she'd bought for John as he walked into the kitchen.

"You look nice," she said, admiring his muscular frame as he modeled the silky blue pajama set she'd chosen for him. "And you're just in time. Dinner is served," she said, walking into the dining room.

The phone rang as they sat down at the candlelit table. "I'll get it," John said. A flash of disappointment passed over Valerie's face.

When she'd shared her plans for the evening with Janice, her friend had warned Valerie that Satan was furious about her plans to revive her marriage. He'd worked hard to destroy it and would do anything to keep her from doing what God planned for her. Was this unexpected interruption his work?

"Uh-huh," she heard John saying from the kitchen phone. There was a long pause. "Yeah. Well, listen. I'm just going to have to take care of that tomorrow. Tally the receipts manually, and we'll double-check them tomorrow morning. Uh-huh. Good-bye."

John apologized as he returned to the dining room. "Sorry about that," he said. "It was one of the restaurants. The computer system is down, and they're wondering how to handle the receipts." He paused. "I told them they'll just have to wait," he said with a half smile.

Valerie thought she could have jumped off the floor and clicked her heels together. She smiled back, then started as the phone rang again. John rolled his eyes as he got up. "OK, after this, I'm turning off the ringer," he said.

"Whoops!" Valerie heard him say. "I'd forgotten about that, but listen," he said, "my wife and I have plans. Tell the fellas I said hey. Gotta go."

"Basketball practice at church," he said in response to her raised eyebrow. "Told 'em we have plans."

"You're right," she said softly, placing a slice of chicken on his plate. "We have plans."

As they ate, John began to talk about a promotion he was up for at work. "I've wanted to be promoted to regional manager since I joined the company," he explained.

"John, if anybody deserves that promotion, it's you," Valerie said honestly. She realized that she truly admired his dedication to his work and the way he worked so hard to provide a good life for her. It had just been a long time since she'd told him so. "If anybody has worked to make himself valuable to the company, it's you," she said. "You're the guy they call in a crisis," she said, referring to his phone call.

He smiled, sensing that her encouraging words were sincere. "Well, remember the time that exhibit from Africa was caught up in customs?" he said, offering her a compliment. "You got through all that government red tape and had those artifacts laid out just in time." She glowed. How long had it been since they'd exchanged compliments like this unprompted?

The conversation seemed to flow naturally as they sat across from each other and talked. In a way, it was like they'd been starved for communication. Like a couple of old friends who were catching up after a couple of years apart, they chatted easily through the main course and dessert.

"You've made some changes in the bed and bath," John said approvingly as he spooned the last bit of cobbler into his mouth.

Valerie smiled. "Yes. What do you think?"

"I like them a lot," he said. He paused as if deciding whether to speak his mind.

"And I . . . I've appreciated the changes I see in you too, Valerie," he said softly. She was moved by his honesty.

"You . . . you look so good to me," he said. "Things are so nice around here," he said, and Valerie knew he was referring to her whirlwind cleaning session a few weeks ago. "And— your invitation—" She reached across the table and squeezed his hand.

"I meant every word," Valerie whispered, blinking back tears and hoping he couldn't hear the nervousness in her voice.

"Do you remember when we used to read the Song of Solomon?" he asked. Valerie felt herself blushing.

"John, those are some of my favorite memories of you," she said.

He pulled her gently to her feet.

"I think it's probably time for some new ones," he said. "I've left a Bible in our room."

Our room. Valerie liked the sound of that.

Nineteen

THE CONFESSION

H ow beautiful is your love, my sister, my bride!" The words tumbled from John's mouth as Valerie sat beside him on their bed, her hand tucked securely in his. "How much better is your love than wine and the fragrance of your oils than all kinds of spices." She shivered with delight.

John cupped Valerie's face in his free hand, his dark, soulful eyes leaving hers only to read from the Bible between them. "Your lips, my bride, drip honey; honey and milk are under your tongue." He leaned forward, inhaling the fragrance she'd sprayed on herself earlier. "And the fragrance of your garments—" he paused and inhaled again—"and the fragrance of your garments is like the fragrance of Lebanon," he said, his breath grazing her ear.

John leaned back and looked at his wife. A long moment passed between them. He kissed her cheek, tickling her with his mustache.

"Valerie, I love you," he said simply. She nodded. "I love you too, John," she whispered.

"I'm so sorry," he said. "I'm so sorry about—"

Valerie placed a finger on his lips and ran her knuckles gently down his jawline.

"John, I'm sorry too," she said. "Please forgive me." She felt tears coming to her eyes, but didn't bother to blink them away. "I was so focused on what we didn't have that I didn't bother to cultivate what we did have," she confessed. "Instead, I almost allowed myself to be lured away. But I don't want to throw our marriage away like I thought I did. You are God's gift to me, my blessing. I love God and I love you, honey. And I . . . I want to try again."

Her husband didn't try to hide his own tears. John set the Bible to the side and moved toward her, enfolding her in his arms. "I want to try again too," he whispered. "Baby, you're my blessing," he said, stroking her hair. "But I want our marriage to be stronger this time than it was before. I want it to be built on honesty, on the truth."

Valerie was surprised at her husband's expressiveness. Even during their most intimate moments, he'd rarely shared so freely from his heart. "I need to tell you something," he said. "I need to be truthful with my wife." Valerie couldn't see John's face, but she saw their reflection in the mirror that hung across from the bed.

John's face was contorted with pain.

"I had filed for divorce," he said heavily. Valerie pulled away from him and buried her face in her hands, trying to choke back the sob that was caught in her throat. She gasped for air.

"Baby, I felt like . . . like less than enough," he said. "When we couldn't have a baby, I felt like there was something wrong with us, something wrong with me," he said. "I've always been able to give you whatever you wanted before, but for the first time in our marriage, I couldn't give you what you wanted most," he said, his voice heavy. "I was powerless. I couldn't fix myself, I couldn't fix you, and I couldn't fix things so that we could have a family. I knew it, and you knew it, and I was sure you hated me."

Valerie didn't know what to say. She didn't realize how deeply she had hurt him.

"I felt so diminished in your eyes," John said. "I remembered the time that we'd dreamed about having a family, the times we'd talked about it when we were dating. I've always thought I would be a father. I never imagined that things would be this difficult, or that this dream of ours would be such a long time coming." His chest heaved with a silent sob.

"And I didn't know how to make it better, Valerie. You were hurting and mad, and I was hurting and mad, and I had no idea what to do or how to help you. I didn't know how to help myself," he said.

She sensed that he was fumbling for words. "And instead of trying to talk it through with you, I—" he struggled to finish his sentence. "I let myself be vulnerable to another woman's attention," he said.

Valerie gasped again as she felt a deep, burning, physical pain in her heart. She couldn't begin to identify the emotions that swept over her. Anger? Grief? Disappointment? Hopelessness? Questions flooded her mind. Who was this other woman? Was she still in his life? Was this her punishment for her dalliance with Curtis? Had they been intimate? She forced herself to inhale deeply.

John sensed her questions and pulled her into a tight embrace. "It was a woman from work," he said softly. "We were working together on a project, and we started taking our lunches together. One day she shared some personal problems with me, and, instead of heeding God's warning in my heart, I began to open up to her about ours—about mine," he said. "I guess I was just wanting a sympathetic ear. I realize now that I should have turned to a pastor or a counselor or one of my friends from church. But, Val, I didn't want to ask for help. My pride, I guess."

Valerie couldn't suppress her morbid curiosity, though she dreaded the answer. She drew back and looked into John's eyes sorrowfully. "How close did you come—"

"To making love?" he finished her thought. "Close, Valerie. Close. I'm ashamed when I think about how close," he said. "We'd decided to get together at her house one evening, 'just to talk,'" he said ruefully, averting his eyes. "That was the day before your invitation came."

John paused and looked directly at his wife. "Valerie, I don't tell you these things just to cause you pain," he said. "And I'm not telling you these things to excuse my actions at all. There's no excuse for the way I behaved."

He took both of her hands in his.

"I felt like my wife didn't want me," he confessed. "I was searching for something we didn't have anymore, something that had been very special to me. And baby, every time you slammed your door, I felt inadequate all over again. And I couldn't keep coming back forever," he said. "My pride was wounded," he said.

"John, I was so cruel," she said, trembling. "I was so cruel. I was selfish and cruel and ugly to you, and I'm sorry."

"The day she and I had planned to meet, there was a crisis at one of the stores," he said, "and I couldn't make our appointment. After that, I decided not to reschedule."

Valerie sighed as if she'd just set down a heavy load.

"Valerie, all that time that I was suspicious of you, I had my own shameful actions to hide," he said. "But after that close call, I ended my contact with this woman, and I had myself transferred to a division where we wouldn't see each other," he said. "Still, I was trapped—I felt trapped—in a loveless marriage. I felt like we'd reached an impasse, and we were going to be unhappy if we stayed married. And I didn't plan on being unhappy for the rest of my life."

He shook his head. "But then I got your note. That note changed everything. Valerie, I have fasted during my lunch hour every day since then. I knew God wanted to tell me something, and I wasn't going to find it out talking to another woman." He paused. "I told my lawyer to shred my divorce file."

John took Valerie's hand again and kissed her fingers. "I've been meeting with Pastor over the last few evenings too. He gave me the name of a counselor we could go to, to work things out." He smiled. "I'm not thrilled about sharing our business with somebody—and I definitely balked at paying for it," he said playfully. "But I want to be your husband, Valerie, and I want to do it right."

Valerie marveled at the turn of events. "I almost lost you," she murmured.

"I almost lost you," John corrected her.

"We almost gave each other away?" she said, a question in her voice.

"We almost gave each other away," he agreed, covering her lips with his. "I won't let it happen again."

Just as she leaned in for another kiss, he pulled away. "One more surprise," John said. "A good one, I think," he said, dropping to one knee and pulling an anniversary band from the pocket of his robe.

"Marry me?" he asked, his eyes searching her face. "I tried to run this marriage my way. I know now who's in charge. I want you to be my bride again, Valerie. I want to go back to the love God gave us in the beginning."

He stood and cupped her chin in his hands.

"Marry me," he said, kissing the tears that were running down her face. "Valerie, I love you so much. Will you marry me? Please, marry me."

She nodded, wordless.

John took her outstretched hand and slipped the band on her finger.

He pulled her to her feet and into his arms.

"We have come before God at this moment to bind our hearts together in holy matrimony," he whispered. "Valerie, as God is my witness I promise to follow Christ as I try to be a husband to you. I promise to put your wants and your needs above my own and all others. I promise to let you reign as queen in my life, and to shower you with love and affection till death do us part." He paused. "Will you take me, John, to be your godly wedded husband, to respect, honor, and stick with me, and to follow me as I follow Christ, loving me only, till death do us part?"

Finally, Valerie could find words again. "As God is my witness, I do."

"May I kiss the bride?" John asked playfully.

"Please, kiss the bride," Valerie answered. And then she quoted her favorite part of their special Scripture to him:

"Awake, O north wind,
And come, wind of the south;
Make my garden breathe out fragrance,
Let its spices be wafted abroad.
May my beloved come into his garden
And eat its choice fruits!"

Twenty

RESTORATION

The ship they were to board loomed over the landscape like a massive, floating hotel. Valerie stared in awe through the windows of the limousine that had picked them up from the airport.

She looked at John, whose pleasure at her surprise was obvious. "I can't believe you kept this cruise a secret from me!" she said, incredulously. "You are something special."

He grinned at the compliment. "Val, you are the special one. I'm going to spend the rest of my life surprising you." He leaned over and kissed her cheek as the limo maneuvered toward the boarding dock. "Besides, everyone knows that after you have a wedding, you go on a honeymoon," he said simply. "This is ours."

As John stepped out of the limo to pay the driver, Valerie thought about all that had happened between them since their wedding night. Her husband had moved back into their bedroom, declaring that he would work to keep their marriage close to God. Valerie had vowed to share her feelings—positive or negative—with her husband in ways that would help rather than hurt their union.

Together, they had rediscovered their love for one

another. John delighted in pampering his wife, and Valerie loved reciprocating. Husband and wife started praying together again. Valerie cherished the times they held hands and brought their needs to God together. Her heart over-flowed with love for John, her John, every time she heard him humble himself before the Lord. And, as John had promised, they started seeing a counselor together to work through the problems that had nearly caused their marriage to dissolve.

She was jolted from her thoughts by a shouted greeting. "Welcome aboard!" said Dr. Matthews. A petite, slim woman stood beside him. "Let me introduce my wife, Ceci."

Ceci smiled. "You look like a couple of people who've been using the fruit of the Spirit," she observed.

John and Valerie shared a look, blushing. "We've come a long way since we attended the conference," John acknowl-edged proudly.

"Sounds like you'll have a lot to talk about at the confer-ence sessions," Dr. Matthews said, handing John a copy of the cruise itinerary.

As they took the elevator to their floor, Valerie marveled to herself. Her husband had to have booked the cruise months ago—at a time when he was unsure about whether or not their marriage would last to this point. At a time when he had needed her shoulder to lean on, at a time when some-one else had offered hers. But he'd still had hope for their marriage. She squeezed his hand and leaned her head on his shoulder.

"What's that for?" he asked, smiling.

"Nothing," she said, beaming back at him.

John swung open the door of their room. Valerie gasped. Before her was the clearest, bluest water she had ever seen. John opened the window and they sat there together, listen-ing to the water slapping lazily against the ship. They watched it crest and foam as it reached the shore.

As they sat there, bathed in the moonlight that shone through the window, John prayed aloud.

"Lord, how could we have doubted You?" he whispered, taking his wife's hand in his. "How could we have thought to turn our backs on You, seeking worldly solutions to our problems?" he paused. "Father, You have taken our disappointment and heartache, and moved and soothed and healed the way only You can. Lord, if we had a thousand tongues, they wouldn't be enough to tell You how grateful we are. Mold us together, Lord, and make us one. Teach us to serve one another. We commit our marriage to You. Let it honor You and encourage others."

Valerie fingered the anniversary band on her left hand, watching it twinkle in the evening light as the ship pulled away from the shore.

"Amen," she said, leaning over to kiss John, her dearest John.

The Negro National Anthem

Lift every voice and sing
Till earth and heaven ring,
Ring with the harmonies of Liberty;
Let our rejoicing rise
High as the listening skies,
Let it resound loud as the rolling sea.
Sing a song, full of the faith that the dark past has taught us,
Sing a song, full of the hope that the present has brought us,
Facing the rising sun, of our new day begun
Let us march on till victory is won.

So begins the Black National Anthem, by James Weldon Johnson in 1900. Lift Every Voice is the name of the joint imprint of The Institute for Black Family Development and Moody Publishers, a division of the Moody Bible Institute.

Our vision is to advance the cause of Christ through publishing African-American Christians who educate, edify, and disciple Christians in the church community through quality books written for African-Americans.

The Institute for Black Family Development is a national Christian organization. It offers degreed and non-degreed training nationally and internationally to established and emerging leaders from churches and Christian organizations. To learn more about The Institute for Black Family Development, write us at:

The Institute for Black Family Development
15151 Faust
Detroit, MI 48223

Since 1984, Moody Publishers has been dedicated to equip and motivate people to advance the cause of Christ by publishing evangelical Christian literature and other media for all ages, around the world. Because we are a ministry of the Moody Bible Institute of Chicago, a portion of the proceeds from the sale of this book go to train the next generation of Christian leaders.

Moody Publishers
c/o Moody Publishers Ministries
820 N. LaSalle Blvd.
Chicago, IL 60610

THE ALLURE TEAM

ACQUIRING EDITOR:
Cynthia Ballenger

COPY EDITOR:
LaTonya Taylor

BACK COVER COPY:
Laura Pokrzywa

COVER DESIGN:
Lydell Jackson

INTERIOR DESIGN:
Ragont Design

PRINTING AND BINDING:
Dickinson Press Inc.

The typeface for the text of this book is
Weiss